Also By Sidsel Munkho available on Amazon.

Hygge – Danish Food and Recipes as Sidsel Munkholm

Nibbles and Bites as Sidsel Munkholm McOmie

Simple Shrimp Recipes as Sidsel Munkholm McOmie

Websites:
http://seapalmtreasures.blogspot.com/
https://www.sidsseapalmcooking.com/

I'm also on Instagram as Seapalmcooking and as Sidselmunkholm.author

Cover Art and Photography
Sidsel Munkholm McOmie

This is a work of fiction.
All the characters and organizations are a product of the author's imagination.

Dedication

The main dog in this book is called Skat – which is the Danish word for Taxes but it is also used as a term of endearment which translates as Treasure. I did call my Chimi 'Skat', because she was not only my constant companion, but also my treasure. She was also a 'rescue'. Not quite like the Skat in this book, but when I got her, she was so skinny, matted and dirty, it was hard to see that she was a poodle. She really did resemble a sheepdog.

To my dear Chimi, this book's for you.

Chapter One

The turkey vultures were clustered around something just inside the tree line bordering the road. And if I hadn't been out collecting heirloom plant cuttings, I doubt anyone would have seen the body before the turkey vultures and other carrion eaters had taken care of it. All we would have found would have been some scattered bones and clothing scraps. And the likelihood of even that would have been pretty slim.

My name's Elle and I've lived here in Berkeys Corner, one of those small towns that were a big deal once upon a time, and now it's tired, faded and small. But it's still a great place to live.

I have a little nursery, selling native and heirloom plants to the big city folks. I often roam the back roads, looking for plants I can transplant and propagate. Back when people buried their loved ones on their own property, the families would plant camellia's, azalea's, crepe myrtle and wisteria around some of the gravesites. Even though many of the gravesites weren't marked with tombstones, due to lack of funds, they marked the graves with plants, and quite often ringed the graves with fences, many of which disappeared long since. You could quite often find where the homesites had been by the proliferation of flowering plants in the spring and summer. Many families also had their own private cemeteries. Where they'd plant flowering shrubs around the graves. Since people did this, I would clean up the gravesites, take cuttings or plant starts from around the cemetery as my pay.

And since I'm out on the roads a lot, I find all kinds of roadkill, which I call into the research place at the university. Someone up there got a grant to tally up all the roadkill, see what animals were losing their lives to the vehicles traveling around our roads. If you're not quick, the road kill gets pulled off and eaten by the alligators, bears, wild pigs, and the Turkey Vultures.

All of which are nature's clean-up crew around here.

This also explains why I had to get closer to what the vultures were gathered around that particular day.

I'd come off of 67 and was on a long driveway, rutty and overgrown. It used to lead up to the Hennessy's, but they'd moved out of the area a long time ago, and the house, such as it was, had fallen in on itself years before.

This particular bunch of vultures looked like they'd hit the jackpot. I counted 30 of them before they hopped away, and some took flight. As I got closer, I could see what looked like rags around the carcass, and I got a sickening feeling in my stomach. And when I got closer, well, let's just say my breakfast didn't stick with me today. The turkey vultures had been feeding on a body, all right, a human body.

I shooed them away as best I could and ended up taking off my shirt and swinging it around my head in circles, scaring more of them off, as I grabbed my cell phone with my other hand and called the local police station in town.

Luckily for me, it was Lisa who answered, being a native here, she could send the police right to me. I told her the old Hennessy place, and she knew right where I was. The old Hennessy place was just one of the many little turnoffs around here that weren't marked. It meant many new people got lost easily, and learned the hard way where the turnoff to Piggott's was, or that is the cutoff to old man Brady's place, or just got lost until someone came along and led them out of the forest. It was also confusing to many people with all the former logging roads that had been cut into much of the forests around here. Many years ago, much of the land surrounding the forest had been under the stewardship of a company which planted slash pines for their pulp content. You could still see the rows of pines, that hadn't been harvested, marching through the forest in long straight lines.

It didn't take too long for the sheriff to come out; again, it was my lucky day to reach people I knew could handle what I had found. Jay was on duty. Jay is my big brother, and he took over when the old sheriff retired. Jay used to be a cop over in Smyrna, but after he got shot, he took early retirement and came back home. He drove his wife Suzanne up the wall for six months until she opened a little dress shop called Threadbare. She told Jay she did that so she wouldn't divorce him. Jay let the former sheriff talk him into running for the office of sheriff then he was asked to be the police chief, and he's been in charge ever since. Suzanne went back to work, and now he's in charge of our little police dept., all 4 officers. We're not a high-crime area, and if we had any more officers, they'd probably trip all over each other.

I didn't have long to wait before I saw his official SUV pulling down the driveway. I had stayed as far from the body as possible while also keeping the vultures at bay.

"Hey Elle, what did you find?" Jay asked as he got out of the car. "Lisa said something about a body?"

I was still swinging my shirt around occasionally, but the vultures kept their distance even while watching me closely. They didn't like having their meal disturbed.

"It's a body all right, but I'm not getting any closer. I thought some idiot had hit a deer again. There were so many vultures here, but when I got up to it, I could see some clothing, and I wasn't about to look any closer."

Jay walked up to the body, squatted down, and looked at it even closer. I stood aways back, far enough, so I didn't have to look.

"Hey, Elle," he hollered, "get back on the phone and tell Lisa to send out the cavalry. Looks like this little girl's been murdered."
He added, "Tell Lisa to call Hank over at the FSIU; he'll want to be told about this one. His number's on my desk."

I was more than happy to make the call, there was no way I was going back there to look any closer. I'd seen enough. And what I'd seen would probably haunt me and give me nightmares for months.

It didn't take much time for Lisa to send out the cavalry, such as it was. Dr. Freitag was our local doctor, and she also did double duty as coroner and rode along with the EMTs when needed or when she was bored, which was a lot of the time. And since she and the EMTs both had to be here, they saved the county some gas money and rode out together.

I stayed out of the way as they all stood around the body and conferred. Finally, I had enough and yelled at Jay that I was taking off and he knew where to find me later. All I got from any of them was an absent-minded wave.

I admit to being pretty shaken up from what I saw,

so I cut my day short and went home. The grapevine had done its damage; Mom was waiting out on the porch when I got there, a pretty teapot and cups already set up on the table. She figured I'd need something, I guess, and she was right; I did. But my idea of something soothing was more like a shot of 120-proof tequila, followed by a nice numbing second shot. And I guess she could see it in my face cause the next thing I know, she was pushing me down onto the chair and heading into the kitchen where I kept my medicinal liquor. I gotta say, when it comes to mothers, mine is the best. She didn't say a word, just poured me a shot and then a second one, waited until I'd downed that one and still without a word, poured a cup of tea and handed it to me.

"Elle", she prodded, " Are you okay?" Since I'm the baby and the first one home, I got the first shot of her mothering. I know her, and she'll be over at Jay's later on, after he has a chance to get home, giving him some mothering, too.

"I am now, thanks to you, Mom." I finally picked up the tea took a sip, and almost spit it out; she'd laced it with whiskey, at least half and half. "What in the world did you put in here?"

"Oh," she said, "I always figure a little Jameson's for shock helps; at least it lets you catch your breath. Did I put too much in there?"

"No, I think you put just enough in here. Why'd you pour me the tequila if you had the tea all ready?"

"The tequila was already sitting on the counter, so I thought you'd rather have that." That was when I knew Nana had been hanging around again.

"Mom, did anyone call and tell you I'd be home right away," I asked, "Or was Nana up at your place again?"

She just looked at me and smiled as she nodded her head. Talk about DEW lines; they don't have anything on Nana. She always knew when one of us needed something: a hug, a band-aid, or a good talking to. And she sure wasn't letting a little thing like her death stop her from keeping tabs on us.

Nana was my great-grandmother; she was into holistic medicine before it became a fashionable buzzword. She was also the local midwife and could see what was wrong with you and tell you if she could help you or if you had to go to the big city for a cure. And Nana was right about 98 percent of the time. She also had 'the sight'; she could talk to the dead.

When Nana was alive, she was pretty good at 'yanking our chain'; she could spin a yarn so good you could almost knit a sweater out of it. And we fell for it, time and time again. And after she passed away, she let us know that she was still around if we needed her. She'd 'yank our chain' and let my mom know which of her kids were in need.

Let me explain about our particular chains. Mom is an artist and made wind chimes for each of her kids, and hung them out in the backyard from the trees with chains. The night Kay's husband died, her wind chimes kept ringing in the backyard and woke Mom and Dad up. No one else's wind chimes even stirred in the breeze, only Kay's. Mom and Dad were up, dressed, packed, and ready to go; when they got the call that Bruce was dead, and they were able to be with Kay within an hour or so. When Jay was shot, the same thing happened; the chimes started ringing as if someone was yanking the chain. And today, I guess Nana was yanking my chain. Otherwise, I'd never have found Mom waiting on the porch.

After drinking Mom's tea, I had to admit to feeling nice and flollopy. Of course, it had nothing to do with the shots of tequila I'd had first. Mom could see I was feeling better and finally said, " Well, are you going to tell me about it, or do I need to wait?"

I told her to expect a visit from Jay anytime, but I'd fill her in with what I knew so far. "I was down that little road that leads to the old Hennessy house. I remembered seeing some camellias blooming there this spring, and I wanted to get some cuttings to get them started." I paused to take a sip of the tea to wet my throat as it had gone dry, "I saw a bunch of vultures by the side of the road; they looked like they were having a party. So, I stopped to see what it was so I could report it to the university." I couldn't help it; I shuddered at what I'd seen.

Mom put out her hand and rested it on mine, so I continued, " There had to have been at least 20 or 30 of them, so I figured they'd found a deer. But as I got closer, I saw one of them reach down, grab a mouthful, and come up with some bright yellow and red rag. He shook it off, and I realized it was a body he'd gotten the rag off of." I got up then and walked around the porch, the image of what I'd seen still vivid in my mind. "So I called 911, talked to Lisa, and told her what was happening. Jay was on duty and out there in just a few minutes, as well as Dr. Freitag and everyone else. I waited around while they looked at the body, and finally, told Jay I was leaving, and that he could catch me at home."

The porch wasn't different from the past couple dozen times I'd walked around it, so I finally sat down at the table in front of Mom again. Skat, my white poodle, had been keeping pace with me. Mom just looked at me, shook her head, and said,

"And?"

She knows me too well; I'm a motor mouth when I get wound up, and I was plenty wound up then. "It reminded me too much of when Lisele died and no one realized she was missing because her good-for-nothing parents were too drunk or stoned to realize their daughter hadn't come home for a couple of days." I turned to look at her and saw she'd poured me another cup of the Jameson tea; she knew that sometimes alcohol helps to numb you enough so that you can process stuff.

" Joe Simmons was the one who found her, and that was only because he saw the buzzards circling that spot. It could have been any of us who ran across her body. We were always around the Millers pond in those days, but none of us had been there for a couple of days."

I paused and picked up the cup and sipped on it; getting drunk wouldn't help, but the Jameson would help a little with the memories. And in my mind, I was back there, with all the wild, wonderful, and horrible memories of that summer 20 years ago.

Millers Pond was a weedy little pond that was still a wonderful place to gather in the summer. One bank was sand, and we would spread out our towels there, sunbathe, have a picnic, and just do all the stuff teenagers do. Lisele was one of us; she'd come whenever she could; most of the time, she was the main caretaker for her little brothers and sisters. Her parents passed out or stoned; they didn't care if any of their kids were around or even taken care of. I have no idea why the kids weren't taken away and put into foster care, but maybe it was one of those things; they were one of us and were taken care of by us, the community. But I digress; the same summer Lisele was murdered was the summer I had my fling with Lee, which resulted in the birth of my son. I'd been drunk on love and hadn't been by the pond for a few days. Somehow, hanging out at the pond wasn't a priority, and in fact, I thought that all the teenagers hanging out there were beneath me. After all, I was in LOVE, and they had no idea how grownup I'd become. Lee was a summer visitor. He and I had taken one look at each other, which did it for us both. I'd been working in town at the ice cream parlor, when Lee walked in, I swear I heard the angels sing. Tall, tanned, and golden, he had just enough bad boy on him that my tongue hung out. He came in wearing a Levi shirt, half unbuttoned, with a gold chain peeking out, long sleeves turned up just past his wrists on his forearms, and tight, tight blue jeans that looked as if they were molded to his body. He made the local boys look like weedy little twerps. All it took was one look and one Pecan Praline double scoop waffle cone, and I was lost. Lee and I were simpatico, joined at the hip when I wasn't working. Lee and I had been exploring each other's minds and bodies, finding out we connected on every level we could imagine. It was a wonderful time for me. Magical in every sense of the word.

And then the call came; Joe Simmons had found Lisele's body lying by Millers Pond. She'd been strangled with the sash from her summer dress. Joe was so traumatized by the discovery he crawled into a bottle of rum and stayed there. He'd been hunting coons, or more accurately, escaping his wife for a few hours (I did say I lived in a small town, we know everyone's business) when he spotted the turkey vultures gathered around something. He just figured it was a deer and went to look. I was always glad it was Joe and not me who'd found Lisele cause Lee and I had been on our way out to the pond that day so I could show him the local hangout.

Selfish of me, but I was still in the first flush of young love, and that would have been a big old romance killer. As it was, our love didn't survive much longer anyway. Summer was almost over, and with it, the end of the summer and the end of the romance.

After Lee left, I found out I was knocked up, as the saying went. Whoops. After his parents stymied attempts for me to contact him to let him know about his impending fatherhood, I decided to just embrace my baby, with or without a father. A few months later, I gave birth to my pride and joy. My family rallied around me, and Nana flat out told my parents that since I was already living with her, she would take advantage of that and show me how to raise a son. And she did.

At any rate, Mom knew I needed to talk out what I'd just seen and experienced. She poured herself another cup of tea and let me ramble on and on and on.

Later that afternoon, Jay finally made it by the house to tell us what was going on. He was hot and looked it. Florida spring and summers can be wicked hot. He wiped off his forehead with his shirt sleeve and accepted the tall glass of iced tea I handed him as I asked "What did you find out?"

"After we got the body back to Doc's place, I made a call to Hank at the FSIU. We're dealing with a murder here, and it looks like someone just dumped the body." He held the glass of tea to his forehead again, trying to get some of the cool of the glass to seep into his hot head. "I swear I could take this shirt off and wring it out. I've sweated so much".

"I know," I commiserated with him, "On days like this, you need a couple of gallons of water and at least two shirts so you can change out for a dry one. I go through a couple myself daily when I'm out in the forest collecting plants."

Jay looked at me and Mom and said, "You're not going to believe this, but it seems Berkeys Corner is the unlucky recipient of the latest in a bunch of murdered girls who've been dumped." He took a long swallow of his iced tea and continued, "My friend at the FSIU told me that they've found three other bodies dumped out alongside roads in small towns like this in three different counties. And every time they've found a body, the media talks it up, and the next body is dumped outside a different town. It's almost like whoever is leaving them is thinking that the police from different townships aren't going to talk to each other. Hank doesn't want us to say anything about finding this girl; he'd like us to keep it as quiet as possible. So, everyone's been sworn to secrecy. The Feds said there is a pattern going on, and if they think this is a safe area to dump bodies, maybe they'll get lucky and see someone who doesn't fit here. They don't want any more bodies, but with this fourth body, but they think there may be more." He looked at Elle and his mother and continued, " I'm asking you guys to keep it quiet as well." I immediately consented, as did Mom. Neither of us could imagine doing anything less.

"In that case, I think we should all have dinner together tonight. You'll want to talk to your sisters about this and let them know what's going on," Mom said, "I'll call the rest and tell them".

Jay and I looked at each other, and I caught the wink he sent me as he said, "I guess you're ahead of me on this as well, Mom. But I know you're right about that. I'll let Suze know. What time's dinner?"

Chapter 2 - Suzanne

Later that night, I sat out on the little porch out back. The air was soft and fragrant with some night-blooming nicotiana, and the midges and noseeums were absent for a change. I sat and thought about what had happened earlier in the evening.

Suzanne

The family had gathered for dinner earlier, just after Jay had talked with their mother, Kay and Emme, and as usual, the dinner table was full of laughter, and people were talking over, under, and to each other.

Suzanne had watched them in bemusement. This family she'd married into was the antithesis of everything she'd been brought up with. Her parents barely functioned as a couple, and if they ate dinner together, it would be when they were out with some of their social friends, not by choice. But this family, this wonderful, loving, supportive family, somehow understood each other. Even though they were talking over and under and sideways to each other, by the end of the meal, everyone had been brought up to speed on the body Elle had found earlier, what the FSIU was saying, and how this could be part of something bigger and worse. Since everyone was still in a heated discussion, she decided to start clearing the table.

Heading into the kitchen with an armful of plates, she was startled into dropping them when she heard a whisper beside her, "*I'm glad you married my grandson; he needed you.*" As she dropped to her knees to clear the broken plates up, she swore she felt a hand touch her cheek lovingly and then heard a chuckle. By the time the family rushed into the kitchen to investigate the crash, she realized she'd had a visit from Jay's grandmother. Something usually just accorded to family members, but this time, Suzanne was the recipient of a visit from Nana, and she knew completely and totally that even though she'd married into this family, they'd also married her. And she finally had the family she'd dreamed of having while growing up. This was her family now – period - end of story. She sat down on the floor surrounded by the broken plates, alternately laughing and crying. That was how Jay found her, and when she explained why she was crying and laughing at the same time, he joined her on the floor, holding her close. And she thought back to how they'd met and how quickly they'd become part of each other's lives.

They'd seen each other when they crossed paths while jogging in the same park in the city but had never formally met until the day she went to get into her car at the park and found that someone had vandalized it. Jay had come up behind her as she stood in shock, looking at the broken side window and the slashed tires. He'd called the incident to the police for her and waited with her until the police arrived to take her statement.

After Suzanne had made her statement and arranged to have the car towed away, Jay offered her a ride home as he lived a block away from her place. She'd accepted the ride, and while they had talked a little on the trip to her home, it was more like small talk on his end as Suzanne had been in shock.

When he called her the next day to see how she was doing, she finally thanked him for the ride the previous day. They ended up agreeing to meet for drinks that evening. She'd never had such an easy conversation with any man. Jay wasn't intimidated by her beauty or the fact that she was well-known as a model; he seemed to like her for herself. And when she found herself confiding in him that she didn't like modeling, that it was just something she fell into, he asked her what else she'd do if she could. And that was when she said she'd like to help people but needed to know how to start. So Jay suggested volunteering. Her parents were horrified when she told them she was quitting modeling and would be helping out at a food pantry and walking dogs at an animal shelter until she found something she wanted to do. And every time Suzanne tried something new, Jay was there to listen. It was as if she'd finally gotten permission to be herself. She'd never had anyone who believed in her as a person before. Her parents didn't, they looked at the surface and never below it. Jay looked and liked what was underneath. And it wasn't too much later that they got married and Suzanne found peace in her life that had been missing. It wasn't long after they got married that Jay had been shot, and when he recovered, he told Suzanne that he'd like to take an early retirement and move back to Berkeys Corner. She was happy to embrace the change, as Jay's family had embraced her happily. Like Jay, they looked beneath the surface and liked her, as a person. Then not long after moving to Berkeys Corner, she told Jay she wanted to open a clothing store. He went back to work as a police officer, and she found herself content in all areas of her life for the first time.

    And now Nana had given her the final approval. So when Jay came bursting into the kitchen, followed by the rest of the family, there was a mad scramble of hugs and cheers when they were told Nana had whispered in Suzanne's ear.

    Although Suzanne hadn't told them all that Nana had whispered to her, she had wanted to wait until she and Jay were alone at home to tell him the rest of the message. She waited while he unlocked the door and for him to do his customary quick scan of the front room even though they now lived in a small town, it was still an automatic thing for him to do. After walking into the room, Suzanne put her purse on the side table.

"Jay", she paused, then continued, "when Nana whispered in my ear, she told me something else, and I didn't want to share it with the family just then." Jay looked at her quizzically. Suzanne then spurted out the rest of the message Nana had whispered in her ear. "Nana told me to tell you that you'd better get busy on the shed behind the house cause we were going to need my sewing room for a nursery."

She waited for a breathless eternity while Jay processed what she'd just told him.

He looked at her as if someone had poleaxed him right between the eyes, "We're what?" he asked, "How is it possible? You told me that the doctor said you couldn't get pregnant."

He paused for a minute, turned to her, swept her up in his arms, twirled her around, and started to laugh. "Trust Nana to let us know like that. I wish you could have met her; she was something." He said aloud, "Nana, thanks so much for the news, and I'll get going on that shed so Suzanne can move her sewing room out there before the baby comes".

Chapter 3

I was scouting the back roads of Tate's Hell a few days after the dinner with the family. I started thinking about the scene in the kitchen with Suzanne sitting on the floor, surrounded by broken plates and food, crying and laughing. Nana hadn't been known for being subtle when she was alive; she'd always let people know when she approved of them or an action they'd taken. Even after her death, she still passed her approval to her great-grandchildren and their spouses.

I knew Suzanne would remember that dinner for a long time, especially with the rest of the news Nana had shared with Suzanne, which Jay had passed on when he called everyone the next morning.

I was excited for Jay and Suzanne; I would never have expected my big brother to become a father. But I knew he would be a great one. He'd been there for me from the beginning when I first found out I was pregnant. While I had appreciated Jay's offer to go and beat the crap out of Lee for leaving me in a certain situation, I hadn't taken him up on it. Even at 17, I knew I was just as much responsible for my condition as Lee was. And when Lee never bothered returning any phone calls or answered any of my letters, I just figured we were in it together; and thanked the heavens for my family.

After Eric was born, Jay and the rest of the family made sure that I and Eric never lacked any kind of support. Or male influence. Eric was my pride and joy and a pretty good kid.

Just then, my attention was caught by a bear up ahead, dragging something off into the bush. I made a note of where it was. After finding the body of that poor girl last week, I wasn't about to go and look by myself; I wanted someone else there with me. Besides which, if you've ever seen a bear head off into the trees, you know how quickly and thoroughly they can disappear.

There was another reason I wasn't about to go and look more closely. It was yellow fly season, and the little buggers were especially vicious this year, and I wasn't dressed appropriately to go out and look.

If you've ever been in the South during yellow fly season, you'll understand why many of us stay undercover or inside while the blackberries are blooming, cause that's also yellow fly season.

That's what I was doing, checking out the blackberries to see how ripe they were. I love to make blackberry jelly and every year; I would bundle myself up, well, long sleeves and long pants tucked into my Panacea Nikes, aka oyster boots, and go and pick blackberries. I've also worn a beekeeper's hat with netting just cause I can't stand to be bitten. I'm one of the lucky ones; I don't welt up, but those bites tend to itch for hours.

So, there were two good reasons not to get out of the truck to check what the bear was dragging off. As I drove past where the bear had gone, I saw what could have been a purple flower. It was past blooming time for the wisteria and azaleas, and I didn't think that Meadow Beauty had quite that large a flower.

So I stopped my truck and got out, braving the yellow flies that clustered around me right away. I could see what looked like a shirt, half buried under some muck. I wasn't about to look further, so I dashed to the truck, trying to brush off the flies so they wouldn't follow me in. I managed to get inside the cab of the truck with only a few flies coming in with me. And then called Lisa at the cop shop.

I asked to speak with Jay, and I guess she could hear something in my voice because she didn't even try any small talk.

As soon as Jay came on the phone, I told him what I saw and where I was. I could almost see him deflate when I told him what I had seen. I knew it could be something as simple as someone dumping old clothes in the forest, but from what I could see of the material, it hadn't been out there long enough to get weathered looking.

It didn't take long for Jay to come out, and he brought Hank with him. Hank is the FSIU guy Jay knew from when he took some classes at Chapel Hill some years ago. They became friends and stayed in touch. Hank had been around a lot as Eric was growing up, but he was one of those people who could fade into the woodwork, almost chameleon like and if you were asked to describe him, you couldn't. He had mid brown hair, regular features, nothing stood out.

This made him a great agent for going undercover. He also had a brilliant mind and ended up doing a lot of profiling for other agents back in the office.

Jay had contacted Hank after I found the girl's body and had been told they were possibly looking at a serial killer and wanted to keep as much of the details on the body and method of death as quiet as they could. So I guess I wasn't too surprised to see Hank there after all.

As soon as they got out of the car, they started swatting at the yellow flies; I think the ones that came out when I first got there had called all the other flies in the neighborhood and told them that fresh food was on the way. Yellow flies suck or drink your blood. If you smack them after they land on you, you'll end up with a bloody spot. Worst part, you usually don't feel the initial bite, and don't realize it until later on when the itch starts. Nasty little critters.

It didn't take Jay long to get some boots on and wade in to look at the purple cloth. Just before he went in, he told me to stay in the truck and not leave. It was hot outside, and I wasn't about to sit and swelter inside the truck of course, with the flies outside, I couldn't even open windows for any breeze, so I added to my carbon footprint and turned on the truck, so I could sit in the cool of the air conditioner. Let it run for a few minutes, and then turned it off again.

It only took a few minutes for Jay and Hank to look at the purple cloth and climb onto the roadway again.

Jay came over to the truck and told me to go ahead and head back into town. He said that there was a trail leading into the forest, and he wanted to get some guys out to follow it in.

"Would you mind stopping in and telling Suzanne I'll probably be awhile yet?" he asked, "I have a bad feeling about this and don't want to leave until we get it all checked out."

"Not a problem," I said, "Anything else you want me to do? Or can you handle it all from here?"

He hesitated just for a moment and then replied, "Just keep it quiet; I'm going to ask the Edmond boys to come out and track with me. They know this part of the woods better than almost anyone else."
He then moved off to go and sit in his car with Hank.

I drove back to town, my head swimming with dark thoughts. I couldn't keep my mind from flashing to the images of the vultures hopping around the body I found. And then to see the purple shirt, half buried in the muck. Selfishly, I just hoped that Jay and the Edmond boys wouldn't find anything. It was bad enough that we were already getting strangers coming to town, and if there were another murder, we'd get even more people, reporters mainly, coming in.

Chapter 4

　　After getting to town, I pulled into the angled parking in front of Threadbare, Suzanne's shop. It had been an unrealized dream of hers to have a shop of her own, where she could showcase the clothes she designed and liked without having to deal with chain store buyers. After Jay had taken an early retirement and driven her up the wall for the first few months, she decided to realize her dream. She opened up Threadbare. And she got a steady stream of customers from most neighboring towns. Word of mouth travels when it comes to good fashion.

　　As I opened the door, she looked up from behind the old-fashioned cash register that she'd found, refurbished and now used. It was sitting on an old desk that she'd also rescued. Her shop was filled with a mixture of classic, vintage, and designer clothes. Suzanne had taken an old run-down shop, which had been empty for years, and had done an incredible mix of rustic and sleek to showcase the clothes she had on display. In one corner of the shop, Suzanne created little tableau's using bedroom furniture and selected clothing items. She changed it regularly, so you felt as if you were getting a glimpse into someone's boudoir. Today's display looked like a teenager had come in and was getting ready to go out. A T-shirt and jeans were strewn on the floor, and a pair of sandals lay half under the jeans. A blue evening gown and a glittery wrap were placed carefully on the daybed, and there were sheer stockings draped over stiletto heels placed carefully to the side. It looked so inviting; it made me wish I had someplace I could wear the dress.

　　On the little knee-hole dresser was a set of brushes and makeup. As I looked at it, I realized that it was almost prom time, and that was precisely why Suzanne had set up this little tableau.

Suzanne was talking to one of our local gossips, Miss Maisy when I walked in, and I could tell from the relieved look on her face when she saw me that she'd been pumped for more information than she was comfortable talking about. It could be challenging to live here. It seemed sometimes as if everyone knew more about your life than you did.

Miss Maisy was dressed in a yellow floral dress that stretched not very becomingly over her more than ample body. Her hair was in its usual champagne blonde bob. From her hair's stiff and shiny look, she'd been in to see Miss Sally at Do Wop Cuts.

Miss Sally doesn't talk much, but she does listen to her customers and occasionally shares a juicy nugget of gossip. And I know she doesn't share with Miss Maisy, so I was pretty sure she hadn't heard about Suzanne's pregnancy yet.
As I came further into the shop, I greeted her.

"Hey Miss Maisy", I asked, "How are you? You're looking good. I hear your grandson's coming for a visit soon," and waited for her reply. I knew her grandson was a sore spot; he was a dancer and appeared in a revue in New Orleans. And the revue, well, let me say this, he could play dress up better than anyone else in town while I was growing up. "You need to bring him in here. I'd like to introduce him to Suzanne; they have a lot in common, and can compare notes.

She mumbled something, nodded at me, hurried up, and left the shop.

"Elle," Suzanne asked, "How did you do that? She's been here for almost an hour, trying every way she can to ask about the body you found. And I really couldn't tell her much at all, but I don't think she believed me".

I laughed cause the best way to get Miss Maisy to let you alone was to ask her how her grandson was doing. I'm one of the few people around here who knows the full story, she doesn't want anyone to know her grandson is the proud star of a Drag revue in New Orleans, even though it is an open secret. Ladd designs and sews his own costumes as well, and I don't know which one is worse for her to acknowledge, his dancing or design abilities.

"One of these days, I'll tell you all about Ladd, but not today." I laughed, "Jay asked me to stop by and tell you he would be awhile yet." Then I sobered up and said solemnly, "I was out scouting for blackberries and saw a bear dragging something off, and when I stopped to look, I saw some clothing off to the side of the road and called Jay about it"

I moved around the shop, picking up a purple shirt on the back of a chair and putting it down again. "In fact, I saw part of a shirt almost this exact color, sitting, half buried in the muck, and it didn't look like it had been there long. When Jay came out, he had Hank with him, and they were calling in the Edmond brothers to come out and try to track the bear or at least follow a trail Jay thought he saw."

I sighed, "I hope it's nothing, but in the meantime, I'm starving. How about you take a lunch break and have some pizza with me."

I looked at her face and added, "After all, you're eating for two now, and you have to feed that baby so it can get big and strong."

Suzanne laughed at that, as I knew she would. She was glowing and more beautiful than usual. "As a matter of fact," she said, "I am starving, and a nice veggie pizza would be great."

I just groaned. I should have known better; I was in the mood for one of Give Pizza Chance's loaded pizzas', but it looked like I was eating healthy today.

Give Pizza Chance is our local pizza parlor. I know, cute name, huh? It was started by a couple of hippies who got tired of commune life, walked into town one day, and the next thing we knew, they'd rented a building and renovated it to make it a pizza place. They even built a brick oven outside to bake the pizza in. And their pizza was good. They had all the usual varieties and made up a few as well. Their Totally Loaded Man Pizza was a 23-inch masterpiece that weighed in at over 6 lbs. It had the best toppings, Pepperoni, Smoked Ham, Genoa Salami, Fresh Mushrooms, Onions, Tomatoes, Green Peppers, Black and Kalamata Olives, Italian Sausage, Linguica Sausage, and Ground Beef. It had been known to feed a family of 6 with leftovers. Or a couple of teenage boys. One of their specialty pizzas was called 'The Veggie Head,' which had a mix of Fresh Spinach, Artichoke Hearts, Fresh Tomatoes, Red Onions, Feta Cheese, and Mozzarella Cheese, plus whatever other veggies they felt like putting on there that day. You never knew exactly what you'd get on the pizza, but it was always good. The Mozzarella cheese they used to top the pizzas was made fresh in-house every couple of days, as was the sauce they topped the pizzas with.

They had an old jukebox loaded with classic music from the 60s; nothing later than 1970 was played on it, and the walls were covered with posters and other artwork celebrating the 60s. They also had an interesting collection of sayings written on 3x5 cards or scraps of paper and thumb-tacked to one of the walls. There were some gems tucked in among the more predictable sayings.

Once a year, for one day, they sold pizzas for whatever you thought they were worth and then donated the entire take to a local charity. And we all got behind on it. They would make more money in that one day than in any one day during the year. Most of us would pay double the usual price for our pizza because we knew it would go to a good cause. Although some cheapskates paid pretty much nothing, it all evened out quite well.

I grew up eating their pizza, and they were just as good now as when I was a kid, even though their kids now ran it. Who just so happened to be about my age. I waved to Moon as we walked in; he was the one tossing the pizzas today, and his sister Sunshine was in the back doing the cooking. The usual tang of tomato sauce was in the air, the good yeasty smell of beer and bread baking. Star was at the register, trading insults with their other brother, Zuma.

Zuma didn't work there; he just liked coming in and hassling his siblings every day. And they liked hassling him back. I mean, when you have a bunch of hippies running a pizza joint, and one of the offspring becomes an accountant and joins the establishment in any other family, it could have caused a rift. But not for them. Zuma was loved for who he was, and besides, while his sibs might have worked in the restaurant, he kept the books for them, which took a load off of their shoulders. It didn't hurt that his husband was a chef and loved to come up with new dishes for the restaurant.

Suzanne and I found a table up against the wall, just under one of the many posters of Haight-Asbury in the 60s, and listened to Star and Zuma, who only interrupted their sparring long enough to ask what we wanted. If I'd come in alone, Moon would have built me a Totally Loaded, but he knew Suzanne would probably not go for that.

"Can you make a 15-inch Veggie Head?" I asked, "Suzanne wants veggies today". Moon nodded, picked up a dough ball, and started to work it. "You want the regular veggies or anything special?" he asked as he turned the dough in mid-air. "We got some nice Broccolini in today, and maybe some Arugala sprinkled on top?"

I looked at Suzanne and she nodded her head yes, so I told Moon to go for it. By the time we'd finished our order, Star was on her way over with our drinks. I got my usual, half and half, (that's half sweet tea and half unsweet tea), but Star brought something new over for Suzanne. She told her it was an herbal iced tea, because, after all, "Now that you're pregnant, you need to limit your caffeine" Suzanne just looked at me in bemusement and had one word "How?"

All I could do was shrug my shoulders. I guess Jay had maybe mentioned it to someone who told someone else, and word got around. It wasn't as if they were keeping it a secret. That's a small town for you, where the good news makes its way around almost as fast as the bad news.

As we waited for our pizza, we made small talk. I didn't want to pump Suzanne about Nana's message to her, but I was curious. Finally, as Star brought out the pizza, I broached the subject.

"Suzanne, I know it's none of my business, but did

you have any inkling you were pregnant before Nana told you?"

Suzanne looked down into her drink and then up at me and smiled. "I was the cliche' here; I thought I had a bug. For a few weeks, coffee smelled awful, and then I was craving meat, which was strange for me, but I thought my iron was low, and then my appetite came back, and everything in the house sounded good to me."

She smiled, "Jay and I never expected this. I never even tried to get pregnant, I'd been told that I could never conceive, and I'd made my peace with it. Even now, I still can't believe it. I've got an appointment with Dr. F next week, and in the meantime, I'm looking forward to getting fat."

She laughed and shook her head, "A former model, looking forward to getting fat, amazing." I laughed along with her.

"Well, I'm glad you're happy, and Jay was glowing when I saw him this morning; I'm actually surprised he could go to work."

"Well, he was a little late today; he kept patting my stomach and shaking his head," she said, "But I finally got him out of the house when I told him I had to come and open up here. And then Miss Maisy came in to pump me for all the gory details about the body you found. I started wondering why I wanted to open the store so badly."

"I know," I said. "She's lonely, bless her heart. She's managed to alienate just about all of her family, and she was downright nasty when I got pregnant with Eric and told everyone that my parents should have done a better job raising me, something I didn't need to hear back then." Suzanne reached over and patted my hand.

"I'm not sorry I had Eric, he's been a joy, mostly, and now that he's off at college; I miss him," and then I continued, "But I get to spoil a new niece or nephew in a few months. I don't suppose Nana told you what sex the baby is?"

Suzanne just looked at me and said, "Not a peep".

We'd managed to eat most of the pizza as we'd been talking, and by the time we finished eating, the restaurant was filling up. Suzanne had to go back and open the store, and I had to go. I still had to finish my route and prepare for my shift at the bar. I often help out at Fred's Place, wait tables, and man the counter at the off-license when they're short-staffed, aka working there. Living in a small town, you sometimes have to do many odd jobs to make a living.

Chapter 5

Eyes were watching Elle as she left Jay and Hank to drive back into town, and what was behind those eyes would follow her later. The darkness behind the eyes kept the blankness of the mind at bay.

After Elle left, Jay and Hank exited the car and got their boots on. Jay had handed Hank his spare pair of gum boots as they left the office with the admonition that if they needed to wade in anywhere, they'd need proper footwear.

Hank grabbed the bug spray, sprayed himself liberally, and then handed the can to Jay. Jay took it, and even though he knew it wouldn't do much good for the yellow flies, he figured it wouldn't hurt to add another layer of protection.

Both men were already wearing long-sleeved shirts and long pants as protection against not only the yellow flies but all the barbed plant life they were likely to encounter. Between the blackberry vines, Cats Claw, and other barbed plant life, walking through the swampy parts of the forest could be hazardous.

Hank motioned to Jay to proceed in front of him, but since both men were well-schooled in observation when Jay stopped abruptly and pointed to an overhanging branch from an oak tree, Hank stopped as well.

"Hank, take a look at that," he said, pointing up, "does that look like a necklace?" He went forward until he could get a little closer and used the camera to zoom in on the item and take a picture. He then looked at the picture he'd just taken using the zoom-in feature on the camera. "Hank, get over here," he called, "you have to see this," as he handed the camera over to Hank. There, hanging from a small branch, was a little silver beaded necklace, the kind that were tossed out during a parade from a float. It was still bright and shiny and hadn't been there for long.

Jay got a sinking feeling in his gut, the same fluttery feeling he'd gotten the day he'd been shot, and felt as if someone was watching them. Then the feeling went away as if a presence had left. Jay shook his head, and continued, "Hank, I want to go and check out that shirt before the Edmond's get here. Those boys are great trackers, but I think we can find our way back to the road for right now," he added, "are you up for it? And let's leave that necklace there until we check out the shirt."

Hank nodded his assent, and they began walking in. The purple shirt that Elle had seen was just a few feet in, and it didn't take them but a minute to reach it. As they got closer, a breeze kicked in, and the unmistakable stench of decomposing flesh hit them. Jay had already taken several pictures of the shirt and surrounding areas, so both men hurried up a little. By the time they got to where the shirt was, the breeze had died down again, and it was that particular hot and still that a southern day gets as a storm is coming in.

Jay reached into his pocket, pulled out a pair of nitrile gloves, and put them on. Hank reached into his pocket and followed suit. Both the men were too well trained to pick up evidence without proper precautions.

As Jay reached for the shirt and bent down to pick it up, they suddenly heard a staccato noise, and both men jumped. Jay then motioned to a nearby dead-fall tree, and Hank saw the Pileated woodpecker busy mining for a tidbit within the tree. Jay shook his head in amusement and then pulled on the shirt half buried in the mud but quickly let it go. Something was inside and moving. As he looked closer, he saw the marks that decomposing body fluid leaves on material—something he'd seen before.

He carefully peeled back part of the cloth to reveal what, at first glance, was an arm, but when he looked at it a little closer, he could see a mass of squirming maggots busily engaged in devouring the remains of some animal.

"Hank, you need to look at this," Jay said, "Someone put the skinned body of a small animal in here."

As Hank came closer, he suddenly felt as if he was being watched as well, but the feeling went away quickly, and he crouched down to look at Jay's find. "Any idea what kind of animal that is?"

"From the size, it's probably a rabbit, but it could be a squirrel as well. We need to get it out of the shirt before we can look at it closer," Jay replied, "But I don't want to disturb it yet; let's go a little further in and check it out."

Both men got to their feet and walked a little further on. They were following a bear run. A path bears make and use traveling through the forest. Jay kept an eagle eye out for snakes; even though they were wearing boots, he still didn't want to see one. He hated admitting that they gave him the creeps. He could face a man holding a gun but heartily disliked snakes. A dislike that had followed him from childhood when he'd been chased by a local bully swinging a dead snake around, which had then wrapped itself around his head. Luckily for him, the bully's father had seen it, and the bully got a whipping. A part of Jay still felt a little guilty about the whipping, even though the larger part of him thought the boy served it.

As they got a little further in they could see some trail, like someone or something had been dragging a heavy object through the forest. The vegetation had been crushed, and leaves and twigs were broken and bruised along the path. But it wasn't a fresh trail; the leaves were browned and dry.

"Hank, I want to go in a little further here. Can you make your way back out to the road and keep an eye out for the Edmond boys? They should be here shortly, and I want to poke around a little here before they muck up the trail more." Jay paused momentarily before continuing, "I don't want to go too far in, but something's been dragged through here."

Hank nodded and started back out towards the road. "I'll get the evidence bags out of the car and meet you back here when the boys come," he said. We'll want to get the remains back to the lab and see what we can learn from them."

Jay kept going on the trail. About 50 feet in, the trail suddenly opened into a clearing after curving around a little, and Jay abruptly stopped. Ahead of him were buildings, rude shacks that had fallen in on themselves for the most part, but there were still two of them somewhat intact. And there were paths worn into the vegetation around the remains of the broken-down shacks.

Jay backed up a little; he didn't want to be spotted if there was someone there, and in fact, he didn't want to explore it further, at least not without someone knowing where he was and with some backup. He then returned the way he'd come with much more caution. He was almost back to the road when he got the prickly back of his neck feeling again as if he were being watched, so he stopped and looked around but could see nothing. As soon as Jay reached the road, he hurried up to where Hank was leaning on the car.

"Hank, I want you to come with me," he said, "I found out where the trail led, and I want to go and look it over, but before we do, I want some backup out here. There was a clearing about 50 feet further in; the trail I was following curved around and suddenly opened up onto a clearing with a bunch of shacks and a path that looked like someone had hacked out and worn down between the buildings."

Hank stared at him momentarily before pitching forward and falling at Jay's feet. As Jay looked down in horror at Hank, a movement caught his eye to his left, and he turned to look.

As Jay turned, he felt something brush by his face, and a millisecond later, the windshield of the car imploded into a pile of rubble. He dropped down quickly and reached for his gun with his right hand as he caught Hank by the upper arm with his left hand and dragged Hank back with him as he sought shelter behind the car. Seconds later, there was another whomp as something else hit the car.

Jay looked down at Hank to see where he'd been shot, but couldn't see any signs of a bullet hole. However, there was a big yellow mark on the side of his face and no sign of blood. Hank groaned and then started to sit up.

"What happened?" he asked, "I saw you come out of the bush, and you were saying something about finding a path, and the next thing I knew, I was back here, laying on the ground, and my head and shoulder hurt."

Jay replied," I have no idea; just as I got up to you,

you fell forward, right at my feet. I felt something go past me, and the windshield was toast. I just grabbed you by the shoulder and dragged you back here." He continued, "I want to go and check it out, but I'm going to call it in first; you need someone to look at your head."

Jay stood up cautiously, keeping his head below the top of the car, and started to scan around the area. Just then, a man came running out from Jay's path into the woods. His plaid shirt was flapping open over an undershirt, and his shorts were barely staying up on his skinny body. He stopped for a second, panting, his eyes scanning the car as he shouted.

"Are you guys OK? I'm sorry the traps got you; I'll explain everything. Oh God, please tell you you're not hurt," he babbled on. "I knew I should have checked the lines earlier, but I was trying to get my data recorded before I did it." He held his arms out to the side and pleaded, "I'm not armed, and you're safe; please tell me you're not hurt."

Jay stood up slowly, looked at the man in total bemusement, and said, "Delbert? What in the world are you doing?" He couldn't believe his eyes; the man who'd come running out on the path was Delbert Hawks, a former town resident. Just then, Hank stood up, with the same inflection in his voice, "Dr. Hawks, what are you doing here?"

Looking at Hank in amazement, Jay turned and asked, "You know him?"

Hank replied, "He's one of Chapel Hill's best forensic researchers. He's one of the guys we go to when we find a body and need to figure out how long it's been dead and where the person died. How do you know him?"

"We grew up together," Jay said, "and the last I heard, he'd gone off to university and became a doctor, and he never came back but once in a while after that."

Hank shook his head, winced, and then said. "It really is a small world".Jay looked at him and told him they needed to get him looked at, and then they could all get caught up. Delbert looked over at Jay and said, "Um, I am a doctor, you know, and um," he continued, "I can take a look at Hank if you want?" he said humbly. He then looked at Hank, had him blink, and hold his arms out to the side, and then had him touch his nose with a finger from each hand.

"I think you're fine, but if you have a headache, go ahead and take something for it later," he said, "I'm used to looking at people who are already dead and can't feel anything, but, umm, I'd go see a live people doctor if you're not sure. "

Jay looked at Delbert and shook his head. Delbert was still the same mix of brash and uncertain as he had been when he'd been at school with Jay.

By the time Jay reached the tow company to arrange for his car to be towed into town, Hank was feeling better, and Delbert had offered to come into town later on and fill them in on what he was doing out in the woods.

Chapter 6

By the time Jay and Hank got back to the office, I'd already talked to Suzanne and found out that Jay and Hank would stay in town to discuss what they'd found. They also wanted to discuss why and how Delbert was involved.

Since I didn't get the pizza fix I wanted when Suzanne and I had lunch, I picked up a Totally Awesome Dude pizza, otherwise known as an Awesome, and brought it with me to the cop shop. I figured out that if I showed up with dinner, they would have to let me stay to help them eat it, especially since I got the 23-inch size.

I pushed the door open with my foot and let the aroma of the pizza precede me. By the time I got inside all the way, Jay had cleared a spot on his desk and was telling Hank where to find the paper plates and napkins. It was common for us to split a pizza in his office, and I supplied him with plates and napkins. I'm just girl enough that I don't want to put a slice of pizza on a paper towel, especially when the paper towels are kept in the bathroom. Hank's mouth dropped open when he saw the size of the box I was carrying. I don't think he'd ever seen one of the Totally Awesome ones, this big. It was a little large, but I knew my brother, and between us, we could make a reasonably good-sized dent in it, and any leftovers never went to waste with the other guys there as well.

"I come bearing food, and I want to find out what all you guys saw in the woods, but not until we've eaten, K?

Jay just looked at me and laughed while Hank's mouth finally snapped shut.
"I don't think I've ever seen a pizza box that big," he

asked. "How many families can that feed?"

Jay replied, "I've seen Eric and one of his friends eat the whole thing. But it usually feeds a few more people than that. And Elle, it's a good thing you brought the big one cause Delbert's coming in to fill us in on what he's doing out there. We should go ahead and eat while it's hot. You didn't forget the 'pencil shavings', did you?" I reached into my pocket and pulled out the bottle with the red pepper flakes. I'll never know how Moon knows when Jay's out, but he seems to know when he should replenish Jay's stock. I think Jay puts it on everything, including his cereal.

Hank went over to Jay's little fridge and grabbed us all a root beer, and we sat down to eat. Delbert strolled in by the time we'd reached the midway point in the pizza. It wasn't the first time I'd seen him since he'd left town to go away to college. He'd changed a little but still dressed the same, and I swear he was still wearing the glasses he used to have. He'd had a habit of pushing them back up on his nose with the back of his hand, then taking them off and rubbing the lens on his shirt sleeve. A mannerism I found adorable and which led me to a very brief 5-minute crush when I was a teen. But then I met Lee, and Del faded into the background, along with everyone else.

"Del, good to see you," I said, motioning to the pizza on the desk, "We saved you a couple of slices of pizza if you're hungry."

Del just goggled at me for a second, hurried up, slid a chair over from the other desk, and dug into the pizza. But before taking a bite, he looked at Hank and asked.

"How are you feeling? Any dizziness or blurred vision? I'd hate to report back that I took out a fellow agent."

I'd just taken a bite of my third slice of pizza, so I had to hurry up, chew, and swallow before I could get the words out. "What do you mean, fellow agent? I thought you were a doctor. When did you join the FSIU? " as I looked over at Jay, I could see this wasn't news to him. And I was happy I hadn't given into my impulse and gone straight home. I had wanted to find out more about what I saw out on the road and what, if anything, it had to do with the body I'd found earlier. I was in the right place to do so. I had not only my brother but also Hank and now Delbert there.

Delbert hadn't changed that much; he could still eat and managed to eat his share of the pizza. He still pushed his glasses up with the back of his hand and then wiped the lens on his sleeve. It wasn't as endearing now as it was once upon a time.

While Del finished eating, I started thinking about how long it had been since I'd seen him. I couldn't remember him coming into town, but a few times after he left. I'd see him out in the forest occasionally, and I had only really talked to him a few times over the years. But then again, I was busy with my life.

After Jay and Del graduated, I moved in with Nana for my last couple of school years. Dad had taken an assignment in Dubai, and I wanted to stay home, so Mom and Dad had gone while I lived with Nana. I wouldn't have paid any attention to any of Jay's friends at that point. I not only had school to finish, but I also had a baby to start raising. My own life consumed me. I was smart enough to know how lucky I was that I had a great support system with my family. I never had to worry about a place to live or any day-to-day hassles. Nana and I were close anyway. Even after Mom and Dad returned and Dad returned to his 'day job' as he called running his company, I stayed with Nana. By that time, her age was catching up with her, and I was able to take care of her for a change. She also seemed to enjoy having a sometimes, OK, most of the time, rambunctious toddler running around, even if it was her great, great-grandson. Eric knew when to be considerate of Nana, and the two shared a wonderful bond.

    Del filled us in after the pizza had been eaten. He was a doctor and had practiced for a few years but didn't enjoy it. He'd always had an interest in entomology and had gotten interested in forensic entomology after seeing an elderly patient who'd been neglected and had bed sores. The sores had become infested with maggots. A doctor at the hospital had introduced him to forensic entomology after he'd consulted with her on a treatment method. She had recommended that he return to school and learn more about entomology. Del had returned to school but had gotten sidetracked by other aspects of forensic science. He ended up becoming a Forensic Anthropologist. He'd worked with many anthropologists and finally got a job at Chapel Hill training agents on what to look for when they were called in on a crime scene. He'd also worked with Hank on several cases and was the one person Hank would ask for when he needed more information. As to what Del was doing in town, he'd taken a leave of absence from work and was actually doing research out in the woods where I'd seen the purple cloth. He'd kept some of the property his grandfather had left him, along with the old farmhouse, and had his own version of a body farm.

    When Jay and Hank went out and started looking around, he had tried to stay out of sight, not recognizing Jay or Hank at first. He'd also been busy setting up some catapults/traps to scare away the predators, bears and wild pigs who were mucking up his research by dragging it away. He had been trying to figure out if natural versus man-made cloth would affect decomposition. Along with many other aspects of research All of which was a little much to hear, especially after eating pizza. However, Del only went into a little detail, which I was grateful for. I'm not into that kind of thing. So when he had late night visitors raiding his 'research,' he'd rigged up a tripwire, setting off weighted bean bags he'd coated in yellow luminescent powdered paint. He thought that if a bear or something else triggered one of the catapults, the bean bag dipped in the yellow powder would not only whack the bear but also leave traces on the bear so he could see if he had a problem animal. He had also set up night vision cameras, which was how he knew that it was bears and wild pigs who were coming in at night. Somehow Jay had tripped the booby trap, which sent a weighted bag winging its way over to Hank and knocked him out for a second. The second booby trap got the windshield of the car, and the third luckily missed everyone but did leave a nice big dent outlined in yellow on the hood of the vehicle.

When they started talking about the gory details of the bodies and the research Del was doing, I knew it was time for me to leave. I had to get to Fred's Place for my evening shift anyway, tending the counter of the package store. I work there two nights a week and tend bar or wait tables and work the off license when needed.

"Well, guys, it's been fun, but some of us have to work, ya know what I mean", I said as I winked at Jay. "I need to go and talk with some drunks now. Y'all have fun talking shop."

As I walked over to my truck, I got an odd feeling

on the back of my neck, a kind of itch that you get when someone's watching you. But when I turned to look down the street, nothing was there, and the feeling disappeared.

I just shook my head, started up my truck, went home, fed Skat and let her out and drove to Fred's Place, and got my favorite spot. I don't like to park too close, but also, I don't like walking too far when I leave to go home after my shift. I was surprised at how many vehicles were already parked in front of Fred's Place., and down the side streets. It looked like it was going to be a busy evening.

Chapter 7

I got to Fred's just a few minutes shy of 7 pm., but the place was already packed. We don't usually get all that many people in until after eight or so, tonight seemed to be an exception though. Our town drunk, Joe, was holding up his end of the bar as usual, or maybe it was the stool holding him up; sometimes, it was hard to tell. We like to say that our town is so small we take turns being the town drunk, but I think Joe has taken more than his fair share of turns over the years.

I hurried up, signed in, and then started to help Julie behind the bar. She was almost out of ice, so I went first to the ice machine in the back and got ice for her. Fred's isn't that fancy a place; we don't have a nice ice machine behind the bar; the ice machine is outside in the little room by the courtyard. She was also running low on limes and lemon slices, so I grabbed some and started cutting them up.

"Thank heavens you're here. I've been running out of everything; I even had to start using the disposable glasses cause I think everyone has been in for a drink tonight," Julie said, flipping her long blonde hair out of the way. This week, her hair color was blonde; last week, she was a redhead. Julie tended to change her hair color the way most people changed their clothes, almost daily, or so it seemed. "What in the world's going on out there? I heard you found a body the other day, and then Jay got attacked out in the woods and had to have his car towed in. Was it that guy he was with out there?" She asked as her hands built what looked to be a Margarita; at any rate, she was shaking something up in the shaker.

"You have to ask Jay about his car; I can't tell you much," I replied, " What do you need me to do next?" I wanted to sidetrack her cause while Julie's a sweetie, she can gossip better than any Hollywood gossip rag. And she does tend to focus on one thing at a time.

"I need fresh glasses, and can you go start picking up empties? I haven't been able to get out from behind this bar for almost an hour, and you know Fred doesn't want any empties left out on the tables," she said as she turned to get another order going. She could have picked up the bottles herself, but she hadn't wanted to get out from behind the bar to pick them up in case she missed out on some of the gossip.

I grabbed a bin from behind the counter and picked up the beer bottles. And Julie was right, there were a lot. Thank heavens, it was still early. It gets a little rough at Fred's late at night sometimes, and beer bottles have come in handy for bashing heads in. I managed to get most of the bottles and empty glasses into my bin on my first swing through. Some of the ashtrays were full, and I grabbed a stack of clean ones to swap them out on my next pass-through. As I returned to the bar, I had a customer at the package counter and got him a bottle of vodka, then headed back out into the bar to get the rest of the bottles and glasses.

I'd managed to avoid Joe, but he lurched off his stool and headed towards me, managing to get right in my way so I had to stop. I don't mind Joe; I just don't think I've ever seen him all the way sober in all the years I've known him, but when he reaches a certain level in his alcohol consumption, he'll just keep talking to you, and dogging your footsteps and begging hugs from the women. He's mostly harmless, just a pest. I came to a complete stop, the bin heavy in my hands, so I rested it on a table and waited for a moment. He blinked at me for a minute, as if gathering thoughts together through his alcohol haze, and then abruptly said, in a completely sober voice, the sour smell of his beer breath wafting over to me.

"You need to watch yourself out in the woods these days; someone's out there, watching. Be careful." He then gathered himself together and stumbled back to the bar. I couldn't help it; I got a chill down my spine. Joe didn't sound like himself. There wasn't a slur on his words, and he looked downright sober as he said it. When the door opened, I'd picked up my bin and gotten halfway back to the bar, and Della walked in. Joe may have taken more than his fair share of turns as town drunk, but Della had the reputation of being easy and guarded it jealously. She's probably slept with more than her fair share of the men in town, as well as a lot who were passing through. And as usual, the clothes she'd poured herself into were just this side of not quite revealing everything she had. Her red blouse was unbuttoned past the swell of her breasts, and it was obvious she wasn't wearing a bra. She had also tied the tails of her blouse up under her breasts. Her white shorts were more a Daisy Duke; if she wore underwear, it wasn't more than a string. She was wearing sky-high heels; they had to be 6 inches tall at least. As usual, her hair was a cascade of red curls, and her kohl-lined eyes looked sleepy and satisfied. It's a look that most of the men here seem to go for; at least, she never seems to lack any kind of male companionship.

Sorry, do I sound jealous? I'm not, really; Della is my age and still looking for something, and she's been looking for a long time. She and Liesl were best friends, and when Liesl was murdered, Della took a page out of Joe Simmons' book, but rather than crawl into a bottle, she crawled into as many beds as she could. Della sashayed her way into the bar, pausing for just a second or three, or until everyone was looking at her, then she wiggled up to the bar and ordered her usual, a club soda with lime. Della rarely drank; her drug of choice was a man in bed.

I finished putting the bottles into the garbage and got the water going to wash the glasses. Julie was right; she was making a lot of drinks tonight and was totally out of shot and highball glasses. It seemed there wasn't much of a beer crowd tonight, the empties notwithstanding that I'd removed from the tables; people were more into a whiskey or shot mood. Which meant we'd have trouble later on. When the serious drinking started this early, talk turned into discussions, and discussions turned into disagreements, and disagreements into arguments, and then the fights started.

I kept an eye out on the bar and was busy filling the ice and working the package liquor counter I was just glad I could shut down at 11 pm. A lot of booze was being poured tonight, and we were busier than usual. I took a break around nine and called up Jay. I wanted to give him a heads up that they might need to be ready for trouble. I knew the two deputies on duty, but honestly, Rafe and Dennis weren't the sharpest blades in the knife block. If I had called Rafe directly, I knew he would have just dismissed anything I said, and Dennis usually followed along with Rafe. Jay could give them a heads up, and they would listen to him, not to a pesky little woman like myself. Rafe's words, not mine. I'd tell him he had an antediluvian mindset, but I don't think he'd understand the word.

And I was right; I heard it just as I was getting ready to close down for the night. There's a background hum in a bar, people talking and laughing, and the clink of the pool cues hitting the balls on the pool tables. Julie usually has music going, not too loud. But when there's about to be trouble, a hush seems to fall over everyone, almost like someone hits a mute button over the bar. You can still hear everything, but suddenly, one voice seems to be louder than the rest, and the next sound you hear can be fists hitting faces, bottles shattering, or like tonight. That one voice bellows out and seems to drown out everything: music, pool balls, laughter, and talking. And I cringed when I heard it and hurried up and got my cell out. I knew we were in for a major bar fight. I called the cop shop, got Dennis on the line, and told him that we were just about to have some major trouble, that some idiot had called the mascot for the Tampa Bay Rays stupid. And Big Jesse had heard the comment. That was all I needed to tell him.

You can call the Rays any name you want. Big Jesse doesn't care, but he loves their mascot and is prepared to wipe out everyone who doesn't agree with him.

It didn't take Rafe and Dennis long to arrive, but Big Jesse had already picked up one guy and thrown him. Big Jesse is aptly named. He must weigh over 350 pounds and stands about 6'8. His arms are massive, and I've seen him pick up two guys at once, one with each arm, and throw them. I hate to think of the damage he could do if he punched anyone; luckily for us, he just likes to pick people up and throw them. It's not so lucky for the guys he picks up, though. They can end up plastered against a wall or draped over the remains of a table. Just as Dennis approached Big Jesse, Della got down from her stool at the bar and walked up to Jesse. She put her hand on his arm and asked him if he would mind escorting her out of the bar; I couldn't believe my eyes. I figured he would just flick her aside like a bug, but I guess the berserker rage hadn't gotten hold of him yet, and he inclined his head , held out an arm to her and walked her out just like that. I swear the whole bar exhaled a sigh of relief. At least I did.

It took a few minutes, but the noise level returned, and it was the usual Friday night sounds again. I was getting ready to leave when the window I used to close off the package liquor stuck open again, and I was trying to get it unstuck when a man walked into the bar. I couldn't move. The man who walked in was Lee; I knew it, my heart knew it; he was 20 years older, but it was him.

It was Lee.

He was here, in Fred's Place.

Chapter Eight

It was Lee, no longer the golden boy I'd fallen in love with at 17, but a grown-up Lee. He'd filled out; the slenderness of youth was now a well-muscled man. His hair was shorter but still a little on the long side. The jeans weren't as tight, but they still fit nicely, and he still wore his shirts with the cuff folded over once. I saw a gold watch on his left wrist, just like he'd used to wear it.

I didn't know whether to duck and run, yeah, I know, but then I realized I'd bring more notice to myself if I did. So I finished yanking the window down and pushed in the little slide lock to secure it. Anyone else who wanted a bottle would have to get it from Julie.

Luckily for me, by the time I'd finished, Lee had walked further in and was talking to Julie, with his back towards me. I was a coward; I waved at her, mouthed the words "gotta run," grabbed my purse and keys, and got out of the door.

I had no idea what Lee was doing there, and while I was curious, I didn't want to talk to him until I had a chance to think. It had been 20 years since I'd seen him last, and the teenager in me had flipped out a little. My heart was racing, I couldn't catch my breath and I knew if I'd had to talk to him, I would have stuttered and said something stupid.

So I did the only adult thing I could: I ran.

By the time I'd fumbled my keys into the lock of the truck to unlock it, I remembered that I could have just used the fob. I drove home in a daze, the memories in my mind tumbling and twisting. They were so crisp and sharp in one respect, but with the overlay of 20 years of living, dimming some. By the time I got home and got the water on for tea, located the rest of the bottle of Jameson's, and thank you, Mom, for that, I had calmed down a little. I fixed a cup, then took the pot and the bottle out to the little sun porch, breathed in the green of all the plants I had in there, and sat down. Skat, my dog, lay down by me. I'm not that much of a lush, but there are times when a little alcohol, judiciously applied internally, helps with shock. And I figured finding not only a dead body this week but seeing my first love suddenly appear after 20 years were acceptable excuses for having a drink.

    As I sipped the tea, I remembered. The first time I'd seen Lee, I was working the counter in the sandwich shop, and I'd just finished wrestling a new tub of Double Pecan Praline ice cream into our ice cream case. He'd made some smart-aleck remark about a girl being able to lift a tub of ice cream and then had promptly ordered a waffle cone with the Double Pecan Praline ice cream since it was fresh. We weren't busy then, so we chatted while he ate his cone, and by the time he'd finished the final bite, I was in love. It can happen that quickly when you're a teenager. It was not only love at first sight; there was a good, healthy dose of lust along with it. We made plans to meet later on. He was in town visiting his uncle while his parents were on vacation. The only problem was that the uncle was here doing a job and had to drag Lee along. Lee's words, not mine. Lee was left at loose ends while his uncle was working.

    So many memories were flooding into my brain that I could barely sort them out. Our first kiss, the long, intense talks about everything under the sun, the meeting of minds, the first sweet fumbles of intimacy. We were each other's first lover, and the first time was every bit as special as it should be. The long walks, even swimming in Millers Pond after the murder, and how strange that felt to all of us. So strange that most of us never went back. And it wasn't long after that Lee left as well; his parents were back from their vacation and wanted him home so he could prepare p for college. We did write a couple of times, and about the time he stopped answering, I realized that I was pregnant. It's such a cliche, I know. I had no idea I was pregnant; we had taken precautions most of the time. But there it was; I was 17, pregnant, and the father was gone. I tried calling him, as well as writing letters, but he was never home, or at least so his mother said. I tried writing him, but I gave up after getting one of my letters back, torn into small pieces and stuffed into an envelope. I sent him one last letter, wishing him a good life and not mentioning the baby. Nana and the rest of my family were my rocks. And I went on with my life and made it a good one for my son and myself.

    I woke up around 5 am. The birds were having a field day, announcing the fact that the sun was going to be coming up soon, and I was stiff from falling asleep in the old easy chair. But I did feel a lot calmer.

    I got up, let Skat out, and then took the teapot and cup back into the kitchen and put a pot of coffee on before heading into the bathroom to shower. I figured that since I was up, awake, and semi-functioning, I might as well get started on my monthly report to the guy at the university about road kill. I wasn't going to include anything about the body I'd found, though. She wasn't road kill, at least not in the sense of what the university was looking for. This past couple of weeks, I'd seen many armadillo's, turtles, raccoons, possums, and one pelican. That was the odd one of the bunch. Most pelicans stay at the coast and don't venture into the forest, but I had found him smashed into one of the unpaved roads. I hadn't checked it out to see if it was a true road kill, as I'd seen it on my way in, and the carcass was gone by the time I came out again. That was the same day I'd found the body as well. I can't say it was a great week for me.

It helped me to work on the report; I had to concentrate and look at my notes as well as download and attach the pictures I'd taken of the road kill. I used to just catalog the road kill, but the new student in charge of the project wanted pictures. So, I took pictures. I managed to get through the report, and I was starting to plan out the rest of my day when my cell phone started playing 'Who Shot The Sheriff', so I knew it was Jay calling. I glanced at the time, cause even though he was an early riser, he usually didn't call before 7 am.

Chapter 9

"Elle," Jay said, "I don't know how to tell you this, so I'll say this straight out. Lee is in town; he came into the office this morning flashing an FSIU badge. I checked it out with Hank, and it's legit." He continued, "He's here because of the body you found. It fits into a pattern he was following on the west coast. I wanted to give you a heads-up cause I didn't want you to see him before I could learn more about what he's doing here. He asked about you; he knew you were my sister, and I told him I'd pass it on that he was here and wanted to see you."

I thanked Jay and told him I'd seen Lee last night at Fred's but had yet to talk to him. I didn't tell him I'd ducked and run; that was my little secret. I did ask him to keep where I was living to himself for the time being.

After talking to Jay, I promised I would come over later, so he could fill me in. My stomach started churning again. Even though I knew I would have to see Lee at some point, I still had a life here and had to get on with it. So, I decided to make my monthly call on Tate. I usually went out to see him after I filed the reports on road kill, just another of my monthly duties, even if it is somewhat self-imposed, or rather, another of the responsibilities I'd elected to carry on after Nana passed away.

Tate lives deep in the forest in a pen-style cabin built by his father. The old man had lived there before it was a state forest and had negotiated the right to stay there until his son Tate's death, at which point the cabin reverted to the state. Nana was a good friend to Tate and his father; they were both healers, and the old man would gather some of the plants and herbs Nana used. He still collected some plants for a mutual friend who's an herbalist, and tells us where to find the plants. I never knew if Tate had a first name I've never heard him referred to by any other name than Tate. Tate had traveled a lot when he was young, sailing out on freighters and tramp steamers, but he's been back here for more than 50 years, from what I can tell. He ekes out a bare living by carving Santa figures out of found wood, and then sells them in town. He also forages in the swamp for many of his other needs. If you know what to look for, the swamp and forest can provide some good eating.

    I stop by to see him every month and pick up however many Santa figures he has, take them to town, and then bring him back bags of cornmeal, some beer, and anything else he needs if he wants. He also has a pirogue, which he takes to town occasionally but usually just uses it around the swamp here. If he's in the mood to talk, he'll share stories of his travels, which are always fascinating. If not, he'll have left any of his Santa carvings on the front porch, usually guarded by one of his dogs. I know to take the Santa's and any notes he leaves if that's the case.

    Today, however, he was waiting on the front porch for me as I drove in. The road to his cabin is more like a rutted trail, discouraging most people. The only way I can make it in there is to throw the truck into four-wheel drive and take it slow. The dogs were sounding off, as usual. The big old bluetick coon hound the loudest; Blue has a bellow that carries through the woods. Even if Tate hadn't been waiting on the porch, he would have known someone was on their way in.

    I got out of the truck, dodged a couple of freshly minted dog piles, and walked up to the porch."How are you?" I asked, "I'm surprised to see you here this early. Usually you're out and about already. Is everything OK?"

He just nodded at me, turned his head, spit out a stream of tobacco juice, and then said. "There's some folks out here what don't belong."

I waited a minute; I learned a long time ago that when he starts to tell you something, you cannot interrupt him; he will continue on as if you've never spoken.

"I've seen signs out there, not good ones. Big kills drug off into the swamp. They don't look much like animals doing the killing. And what's being drug looks too big for a deer or a wild pig to handle. You need to be careful out here, keep yore gun handy, some two leggeds are trouble."

With that, he got up and went inside. I could hear him rattling around inside, and he came back out a couple of minutes later with a shotgun and propped it up beside his chair. He then told me to come on and sit down. I sat down on the twig chair he kept on the porch. It was the one my Nana would sit in when she came out to see his father and the one I always sat in when I was invited to do so. You could see it had been crafted with skill, and it was truly lovely with the bentwood in a graceful arch across the back. And also quite comfortable. The cushion on the chair was one Nana had made and brought out to Old Tate years before, and even though it was now faded and worn, you could still see the floral pattern of the material from which Nana had made it. I imagined Tate taking it inside between visits, as it would never have lasted all these years otherwise. I waited for him to continue speaking. And while waiting, I sat and rubbed the ears on the bluetick hound. This dog was a particular favorite of mine. I'd found him in the forest a few years before, half-starved, covered with ticks, and wounded from a fight with another dog or predator. He'd probably been dumped after hunting season to fend or not, for himself. So, after putting him in the truck with me that day, I'd stopped to drop off supplies for Tate on my way back into town. The hound had bayed when I stopped, and Tate had been sitting on the porch that day. The next thing I knew, the dog was in the cabin and was being doctored. He never left there again. But every time I came, that old dog would come for a cuddle. It was as if he liked to let me know he was grateful but never tried to leave with me; he would just let out a bay as I went.

Tate finally started talking again. "I've been seeing lights out in the back there, not where anyone lives. None of the dogs have been exploring much, either. You need to watch yore step out here."

I nodded at that, and then I told him about finding the young woman's body earlier that week.

"That was one of the reasons I wanted to stop by today as well", I said, "I wanted you to know about it and to keep your eyes open, but I guess I'm a little late on that."

I got out of the chair to leave, and he interrupted me.

"Before you go, tell me how to get one of those cell phones you always tell me about. I figure I can use the solar panels I have to charge it."

So I explained about the pay as-you-go plans on phones, basically, they're called burner phones, but for him, one of them would be ideal. I'd told him once that if he had a way of charging a phone, he should think about getting a cell phone, but he'd dismissed the idea immediately. I realized afterward that he didn't even have electrical power out there; I'd managed to fit both feet into my mouth simultaneously with that statement. So, my mouth dropped open when he told me he had solar panels. I had yet to learn that he had them or even when he'd had them installed or built, or whatever it is you call it. I told him I'd pick him up a phone in town and bring it to him in the next day. He had a couple of nice sized Santas' carved, so he helped me load them into the truck, and I headed back to town. My head was swimming. I needed help equating Tate with solar panels, much less a cell phone. And for him to be so concerned with what was going on in the forest that he made a point of bringing out his shotgun made me nervous. I always kept a shotgun in the truck and the revolver Nana had given me many years before. Sometimes, you need to scare stuff, but I'd never actually shot a living animal. I knew how to shoot; Jay had taught my sisters and I the basics of handling a gun safely. I'm out in the forest often, but I prefer warning the wildlife that I'm there by banging around. My truck has a lovely rattle in the tailpipe which I've never bothered fixing cause I figure the bears and pigs will hear me coming and get out of my way. I wondered though: was it time to unearth my ancient CB radio and keep it handy?

    My thoughts were reeling, so I was not ready to be in the forest today. If you're not paying attention all the time out here, you can get into trouble, and I'm not talking the two-legged kind of trouble. There are too many other dangers out here that can buy you a little plot of land, and with the way I was thinking, I might become the not-so-proud proprietor of one of them. So I decided that rather than go and check out the old graveyard to see if the crepe myrtle was ready to be dug, I'd head to the little shop that took all of Tate' Santa's' and then get him his phone. If he wanted a phone, I would make sure he got one.

Chapter 10

It was after 10 am by the time I got back to town. I'd driven around for awhile, why, I don't know. I had so many thoughts going through my brain, it was hard concentrating on just one thing. The week had been such an eventful one.

My mind kept coming back to the body I'd found, then seeing Del here, having Hank brought in by Jay to help out, and then the final straw, cherry on top of the cake, whatever you want to call it, of Lee coming back to town.

I stopped in to see Miss Jane, the proprietor of the shop, and told her I had several Santa's for her. She was thrilled. She sells some in her store, but also sells them online and they end up all over the world. She calls them the best of the primitive art. I've been told people keep them on display year round.

I also wanted to make sure that there was enough money in Tate's account with her so I could purchase a phone and get it activated and keep it activated. As I said before, Tate rarely comes into town, and I and Miss Jane have been taking care of his sales and needs for years. He has a bank account, but I have no idea how often he even checks it. If he needs something, I get the money from Miss Jane.

"How are you?" Miss Jane asked, as we unloaded the Santa's. "I imagine that was an awful shock for you to find that poor girl's body. And the way you found it", she fussed, "I just want to make sure you're doing alright. If there's anything I can do, please tell me."

I knew she was sincere about that, she's a kind, kind lady, with a very nurturing spirit.

"I'm doing fine, but I had a question for you," I replied, "Tate was asking me to pick him up one of those prepaid phones, does he have enough on the account that I can do that? And keep it active until he tells me differently."

"He has more than enough for a phone on his account. In fact I think you could keep it going for years if you want. How is he going to charge it? You could even get him one of those smart phones and he can keep up with whats going on in the world."

"Actually, Tate just asked me to get him a regular phone, he said he has some solar cells that he can use to recharge the phone. So that's what I'll do. But, I can tell him about the smart phones when I bring that other one out. I just wanted to make sure he can afford it, and either have you add that to the list or I can, so that it gets paid every month."

I finished up with Miss Jane and headed over to the Dollar General to get a phone. I don't know what we'd do without Dollar General here in town. They tend to sell a little bit of almost everything you need.

And when you have to drive 30-60 miles to get to the next big town where they have big box stores, well, it sure is nice to have one of these right in town. Come to think of it, I think they actually have them spaced out every 15 miles or closer. There are people living here who've not been out of our town in 20 years, everything they need is here in town.

After looking at the phones they offered I finally picked one that said it had the longest battery life along with being able to work on our cell towers here. It then took me a little while to read through all the various plans that were offered. I finally settled on one plan that meant I could prepay the phone for 6 months, and it would give Tate 1000 minutes talk time a month as well as text messaging. I had trouble believing he would need more than that if he'd never had a phone, but just in case, I made sure I could upgrade the plan if needed. I had no idea how he was going to plug the phone in for charging so I got him a car charger that would work on a 12 volt car battery as well as a wall charger. I decided to take it home with me and charge it before taking it back out to him. After I paid for the phone I headed back over to Miss Jane's and gave her the receipt for the phone and chargers and was reimbursed. She asked me to take Tate out some paperwork, went in the back and came back out with an envelope for me.

It was getting on for noon by now so I decided I could throw together some lunch and charge the phone for a couple of hours while I got a nap. I was tired and needed to zone out for a little while. And my poor dog had barely been outside to pee this morning before I left again. I decided that she could go with me when I headed back out to see Tate later on today. She loved to visit with his dogs, and most times when I headed out to see him, she went with me. Skat was another of the 'found' dogs. The dogs that survive being dumped after hunting season or for whatever reason, and get found before they lose their lives to any of the hazards of the forest. I found her cowering behind a bush at the Creery sister's place a couple of years ago. She was matted and so dirty I had no idea what color her fur should have been. I couldn't even tell what breed she was. I guessed that she might be some kind of sheepdog, but after taking her home, getting her bathed and groomed I found out she was a standard poodle. Although she was almost half the weight she should have been, she did fill out nicely. And she's now my constant companion, well, when the weather permits. She's not too fond of hot weather and prefers to stay inside where it's cool if the temps outside are over 80 deg. The tile floor and her are good friends during hot weather. I think it has a lot to do with the fact I found her on a hot July afternoon and her fur was so long and matted, you couldn't tell what breed of dog she was. When it's cooler outside, she's with me as much as possible.

I got out some Bok Choy I'd bought a few days ago and quickly sauteed that with some mushrooms, seasoned it with some sesame seed oil and a little soy sauce and then added some bean thread noodles.

I wouldn't have admitted it to Suzanne, but I did eat somewhat healthy when I was cooking for myself. Since Eric wasn't there, I didn't have to add any chicken to it. Having a teenager in the house was like dropping food into a bottomless pit, they were never full. But at least my food bill was a lot lower now and the fridge stayed mostly full. And there were times when I hated that. Eric would be home whenever he could. He came home whenever he could get a ride back here from college.

After I ate, I stretched out on the bed, and was surprised to find it made for a moment, until I remembered I hadn't even made it in there last night. It didn't take but a couple of minutes before Scat came and asked to come up with me. She was usually happy to just stretch out beside the bed, but I guess she was sensing I needed some company.

I fell asleep, even though I thought my mind was still going 50 miles an hour, but I guess my body knew better than me, cause it shut me down for a blessed 2 hours, until the phone rang. It was my all purpose ring, so I knew it wasn't one of the family, they all have their own special rings. I reached over to grab the phone, and then remembered it was on the dresser, I'd plugged the phone I'd purchased for Tate into my charger by my bed. I was feeling really groggy and just didn't feel like making a sprint out of bed to get the call, so decided to let it go into voice-mail. I wanted to lay there for a bit and wake up, however I fell asleep again. I woke up a little later and decided I'd better get up, I wanted to get the phone out to Tate before it got dark. He'd gotten me a little concerned and with that poor murdered girl I'd found, and how he told me about strange doings out in the forest. I didn't want to leave him without a means of calling out. I got up, fixed a cup of tea and let Scat out again. She'd napped along with me, and was feeling all refreshed and ready to go. I decided to take Tate out some of my Kitchen Sink cookies, that I'd made for Eric and his friends. I was so used to making cookies for Eric and his friends on a weekly basis, and when they'd asked if I could please make them up a care package once in awhile and ship to them at the college, I'd gotten a little carried away and made way too many cookies. I ended up freezing a lot, but there was still a couple of dozen sitting on my counter begging to be eaten, and I thought Tate might just appreciate them. I knew giving them to Tate would do more good for my waistline than keeping them here.

    I'd totally forgotten about the call that woke me earlier and it wasn't until I decided to call Jay to let him know where I was going that I looked at the phone and realized that there was a message.

    When I looked to see who had called I groaned inside. It was Julie from Fred's Place, and I really didn't want to talk with her. I called Jay first to let him know I was heading over to Tate's and then clicked on the phone to hear the message that Julie had left.

"Hey Elle," I heard, "Sorry for the short notice but can you come in tonight? And some guy was in here last night asking about you, I told him you were working the off sale but I guess you'd gone before he came in. He told me he used to know you and wanted to catch up and talk. I told him you were pretty much at loose ends these days with Eric in college and you worked most Friday nights here. Whoops, gotta go, someone's calling in. See you later."

I clicked off the phone, and just shook my head. Julie might have been a good bartender, we all knew she was a gossip, but I was wondering what else she'd told Lee.

I called her back before I left, and when she didn't answer, I just left her a message telling her I'd be in on time and headed on out to Tate's place.

As I was driving out there, I kept an eye out for a wake of vultures, I don't mind admitting I was spooked. That body and Tate telling me he'd seen lights out in the swamp and then asking me for a phone, well. Too many odd things happening for me. I like my life nice and simple, just the way it was.

I made it out to Tates' place, gave him the phone and showed him how to use it. Scat had a great time playing with the dogs and I think Tate had eaten most of the cookies by the time I left. I felt a lot better about him being alone out there now that he had a way of contacting myself or someone else if he needed to.

When I left Tate, I only had enough time to get home, feed the dog, and shower quickly before heading to work. Fred's isn't my favorite place on Saturday nights. They have live music, and it gets a little rowdy. The music is usually decent, and it's loud enough I don't have to make polite conversation. All I wanted to do was sit down and process what Tate told me. After I'd handed him the phone, we played with it a little, including him making a call to Jay, and we'd talked. He pretty much inhaled the cookies I brought him, and I promised to bring him more the next time I came out. But in between bites, he'd expanded a little on what he'd been seeing and what he'd told Jay in the phone call. It was more of what the dogs had been sensing.

They were used to living out in the wilds, so the occasional bear, panther, or wild pig wandering around meant they'd sound off a warning woof and then quiet down. Just before I'd found the dead girl, his dogs had been growling a lot in the middle of the night, and Tate had quieted them down but had gone out to see if he could see what had disturbed them. He'd thought maybe some kids from town had come out to party, but when he walked outside, there was silence and just a light bobbing around and then the light was extinguished. And when I'd come out and caught him on the news, he realized that he may have seen something that Jay should check out.

He was disturbed that maybe the lights he'd seen that night could have been the murderer. I promised to come out in the next couple of days and check in with him, but in the meantime, at least he now had a phone and a means of contacting Jay if needed. And I had to admit to feeling relieved that he wasn't as isolated as he had been.

As I pulled into the driveway, I thought more about the evening ahead and how quickly I could get ready to go. I was due at Fred's in less than an hour, and I needed every minute to shower, feed the dog, and grab a quick bite for myself as well. I managed to make it there in time, and in fact was swallowing the last of my tomato sandwich as I pulled into my favorite parking spot.

As I walked up to the door, it opened, and the smell of the bar wafted out. A malodorous combination of smoke, spilled beer, and sweat. And I knew it was going to be a long night. The loggers were in, and the oyster men were there as well, and between them both, I don't know who stinks worse. For some reason, they loved to come in for a few beers after a long day out in the sun before they headed home for a shower. It was just one of the reasons I didn't like working on Saturdays, apart from the fact that when I do, I start an hour earlier, and finish an hour later. The only saving grace was that I usually got good tips, and they'd helped out a lot over the years with the cost of raising a young boy.

I got in, nodded to Julie, and started picking up empties throughout the bar, trying to breathe through my mouth. It wouldn't take long, and the aromatic imbibers would leave to go home and get dinner, but when you've spent the day out on the water, oystering, a cold beer goes down well. Of course, most of those guys had also been at Fred's for a few hours. They start early in the day, when it's still coolish, and get back in with their oysters before the central heat of the day hits, but it's still thirsty work. So if you add their unique sweaty aroma to that of the pine and sweaty scented loggers, it could get really aromatic in Fred's by 6 pm.

It didn't take long before they all started drifting out, and the evening crowd came in. At least most of that crowd had showered before coming in for a drink. I was behind the bar, cutting up some limes and lemons for the drink station for Julie, when Lee walked in the door.

I was so tempted just to cut and run, but the grownup in me took over, and I stayed put. I had no idea how to react to Lee. He was my major teen love, the father of my child, but we hadn't seen or spoken in almost 20 years. The last communication I had from him was the message his mother had relayed when I called him to ask why he hadn't replied to my letters. She'd told me that Lee had said to her that I was being a pest and wouldn't stop bothering him and that he just wanted me to leave him alone. The memory of that devastating phone call and my feelings back then helped me to steel myself.

Lee walked up to where I was standing behind the bar and just stood and looked at me. I looked back at him. He was still a blond god, but a grownup one, and he did look good. I'd ducked and run so quickly the night before that I hadn't looked at him closely. I guess I was hoping to see some softening around the waistline on him, but he just looked great. He'd filled out; the boy was now a man. He still wore his long-sleeved shirt with the cuff rolled up on his forearm, and his jeans were snug, showing off his muscular legs. But when I looked him in the face, he had changed, not for the better. While his eyes were still a gorgeous dark blue, they looked guarded and not open anymore. And while his mouth smiled, it was just a little. The wide-open grin he used to have was gone. The smile now was that polite one people put on their faces when being introduced to someone they're not sure they even want to meet.

"Hi Elle, is there any chance we can talk? I need to ask you some questions about the body you found. I'm sure Jay has already filled you in on why I'm in town and who I work for now", he said. I was so shocked that those were the first words out of his mouth that I did the polite stranger smile back at him and replied.

"I'm working right now; we can talk tomorrow; I don't get any breaks when I work here on Saturday nights."

"That's fine. Meet me at Jay's office tomorrow morning at 8 am. I want to find out what exactly you saw, where you were, and anything else you can tell me."

"8 am? I don't get home until two or later, and there's no way I will get in there by 8." I was a little po'd by that; his expecting me just to jump and run into the office; there was no way. I usually got to bed after 3 am when I worked Saturday nights. By the time we close, clean up the mess, eject the last of the diehards, and I get home, I need to decompress for at least an hour. Lee didn't look happy when I told him that.

Just then, Julie called me and I had to go and get some drink orders out. I left Lee standing at the bar, and got so busy the next little while, that even though I was aware he was still there, I didn't go near him. I let Julie take care of him. The music started by 9 and the band we had that night made up for their lack of talent with enthusiasm and volume, and by closing time, my head was splitting. I'd gotten glimpses of Lee from time to time, but had kept my distance, which wasn't as hard as it sounded. We have a little courtyard outside where the band usually plays and I managed to stay out there. I did notice that Della had come in at one point and she'd wrapped herself around Lee right away, but that was the last I saw of her. Which was kind of odd, as she usually found a companion and stuck with him the whole night. I had no idea what time Lee left, and was just thankful when the band finally sang their last song and blessed quiet blanketed the bar. I'd gotten a lot of the side work done already so it was just a matter of a few final things, and I was out of there. We'd been so busy, we'd actually run out of Natural Light beer, and had to substitute another brand. However, I don't think any of the drunks could taste the difference by that time. I pulled my phone out and checked it for messages, as soon as I got in my car, force of habit, as Eric always texted me when he got home.

And I saw that Tate had called, just a minute or so before I checked my phone. He hadn't left a message, but just the fact that he'd called with his new phone was enough to worry me. I called Jay but Tate had woken him up already, and had told him he'd already called me. Jay said Tate wanted us to come out to his place so I headed on out to Jay's house to pick him up, since I had the truck out already, and with the road into Tate's place needing something with a four wheel drive, my truck was the logical vehicle. By the time I got to his house he was waiting at the curb with a thermos of coffee and some cups in one hand, a rifle slung over his shoulder and with a pair of boots in his other hand. I do love my brother, he knew I'd been working at Fred's and would appreciate the shot of caffeine to keep me going.

"Can we shoehorn Hank in here too? I have a bad feeling about this. Tate sounded pretty upset, he said he'd heard screaming and saw lights awhile ago. And his dogs were sounding off too, which he said was unusual."

"No problem, is he staying over at Miz Bert's place?" I asked as I pulled the truck into a tight turn and headed back down the road. Miz Bert is our local hotel/motel/rooming house. She rents rooms out by the day, week, or even the month. She also has a couple of little cabins in the back which she also rents. They're the remnants of a larger auto court from the 40's. She and her late husband bought the auto court and the old rooming house and were rehabbing them when he fell off the roof and died a few years back. She finished off the rooming house and now calls it Bertie's Hotel.

"He's actually staying in one of the back cottages. He said some of Miz Bert's guests were being a little too friendly, so he moved out of the rooming house. By the way, Hank said some more FSIU guy's are coming to town, seems the girl you found might be the victim of a serial killer they've been tracking for awhile now. The MO seems to be similar, just wanted to give you a heads up".

"Lee came into the bar tonight and wanted me to meet him at the office tomorrow at 8 am. I told him no way, that I would call him when I got up. I need to talk to you about him, but it can wait until later. I looked out the windshield then and saw a person waiting in front of Miz Bert's place.

"Looks like Hank's out there waiting for us already." I was glad of the crew cab in the truck tonight because Hank had a large duffle bag with him and a rifle on a strap slung over a shoulder, and it was easy enough to put him and the bags in the back, along with the rifles. I took advantage of the stop to pour myself a cup of the coffee Jay had brought and after taking a sip, knew that Suzanne had made it and not him. It was drinkable, strong, but good. I'd figured out that I'd just suffer through the coffee if Jay had made it, cause, gee, caffeine is one of the 6 food groups.

"Did you make Suzanne get up and make coffee, big brother?", I asked. "I'll have to thank her later on."

Jay just shook his head, "She was awake already, she knew you'd just put in a full day as well as working the night shift and figured you'd need some caffeine."

"Well, I appreciate it, but I'm really worried about Tate. Mind if I break the speed limit going out there?"

"Nope. But, do you mind if I drive your truck? I think I can handle it."

I didn't mind a bit, and hurried up and traded places with Jay. I let Hank stay in the back, but knew Jay could get us out there as fast as I could, and he'd also had the advantage, I hoped, of getting some sleep. Tate doesn't live that far out, but it could take us close to an hour to get there, as the forest roads weren't all that great, and you couldn't drive down some of them that fast. Not to mention the fact that there were all kinds of animals out at night as well and hitting a bear or deer was not a fun thing to do. I knew that one for a fact, as I'd run into a bear once, and he left a nice big dent in my front fender and broke my headlight casing as well. Luckily, he'd managed to run off, so I knew he wasn't that badly hurt. It had been years since I'd been out in the forest at night and I'd forgotten how dark it could get. The only lights we could see were the headlights on the truck and Jay had turned on the high beams, as well as the fog lights and from time to time we'd see deer as still as statues on the side of the road, then watch them go bounding off into the forest. I just sat and watched and listened to Jay and Hank talk about where we were going, and let Jay fill Hank in on Tate and his life. Nana had taken all of us out with her to see Tate from time to time, as well as Old Tate too. So we all knew him and his father.

"Hey Elle, I need you to tell me when we're getting close to the turnoff to Tate's place", Jay interrupted my reveries. "I hate to admit it, but it's been awhile since I've been out to see him."

I sat up and started looking out through the windshield. "OK, it looks so different at night, but I can do that" I started looking for the split pine tree, which was how I knew I was getting close to the turnoff to the cabin. A few years back a tree had fallen onto the pine tree, which bent over and eventually split and broke.

I saw the tree coming up and told Jay we were getting

close.

"How good is your night vision?" he asked. "I'd like to shut down the headlights and creep down the road. I know it's pretty rough, but I'd like to try."

"OK, we can try, why don't you stop for a second and turn the lights off now, give us a chance to get our eyes used to the dark. The turn off is about 1/4 mile further. You can see the gap in the treeline there."

"Got it, turning the lights off now"

"I've got a pair of night vision goggles in my pack, if you want them Jay." Hank said from the back seat. "Might make it a little easier to go down that road."

"I should have known you'd have some kind of goody in there" Jay replied, "You sure you weren't a Boy Scout once upon a time?"

"Got any more goggles in there Hank", I asked, "it might be kinda nice if we can all see in the dark."

Hank laughed as he handed me a pair as well, "I knew you were coming, so I threw in an extra pair. And no, Jay, I was never a Boy Scout, just a Ranger."

I took the goggles, and was a little surprised that they looked more like a pair of monoculars than anything else.

I put my goggles on and immediately the whole world turned green. Jay had already turned off the lights, before we put the goggles on. He put the truck back in gear and we started down the road to Tate's place.

For some reason the road felt a lot rougher at night, and Jay let the truck creep down the lane at a low speed. I was fascinated with the goggles I was wearing, this was the first time I'd worn a pair and I was surprised at how well you could actually see. Although the single lens made it a little tricky.

"What else do you have in your goody bag?" I asked Hank, "These are pretty darn cool."

"Nothing too much else, Elle, those goggles take up a lot of room."

"I have to ask, why did you have goggles with you? I know Jay called you about that body, but why bring the goggles and, also just what else did you bring?"

"I just brought a few necessities, it's been awhile since I've been out in the field, and I didn't know just what we'd need."

We'd been chatting as Jay was driving when he suddenly shushed us.

"Look, there to the side. I think it's a panther." I looked and sure enough, it was one. They were such secretive animals that you rarely saw them, but this one had obviously been out hunting as it had some kind of small animal in its mouth. As we watched it loped off into the woods. We were almost at the cabin by then, and as we came around the bend we could see it. Tate was out on the porch with the dogs, waiting for us. The goggles let me see him clearly as he nodded sharply as if he was pleased with what he saw. The dogs were used to the sound of my truck so they didn't even sound off.

Jay came to a stop and cut the motor and we all clambered out of the truck, Tate motioned to us, to come in to the cabin and we quickly walked up the steps. There was a glow around the door, and it showed up very brightly on my goggles. We took off the goggles and went inside with Tate. He didn't even greet us before saying.

"Well girl, good thing you brought me that phone today. I saw some lights off to the west and then heard some girl caterwauling away. And there shouldn't be anyone over that way. Only thing out that way is the old cabin the Mathrey's own."

He motioned to Jay and Hank and then to the chairs sitting each side of a faded, lumpy looking easy chair.

"Sit down, we need to talk" and then flipped his hand towards Hank, added, "I don't know you but if these two brought you out here, you must be alright'. Jay then made the introductions and Tate sat down.

I sat down in one of his bentwood chairs, and found out where the cushion Nana had made resided when it wasn't outside. Blue came over and rested his head on my knee and I gave him his cuddle. And then watched as the rest of the dogs walked over to Hank and Jay and sniffed them both, they then looked at each other and nodded as if to say that it was all right, and went and laid down on one of the hand tied rugs.

"Now, what can you do tonight? I see you brought some NVD's with you." Hank and Jay looked at each other when Tate called the goggles by their correct name.

"Did you bring any boots and what about guns? I have an extra rifle, but I want my own gun if we're going over there."

Jay looked over at Hank and nodded once, before he said. "I have boots, and a gun, Elle has her gun in the truck and I bet Hank brought a couple in his go bag as well. If you can lead us over in the general direction, I bet Elle will let you use the NVD she had on, and we can go take a look." Jay then looked at me and continued, "I think Elle can hold her own but maybe she could stay here and monitor us. I can call her and leave my phone on so she can hear what's going on."

Just then Hank reached into his bag and pulled out a couple of walkie talkies, and handed one to me and another one to Jay. I couldn't help it, I started to laugh. Which eased the tension in the room a little.

"Any other goodies in there? I said. I have to ask."

"Just Betsy", Hank said as he pulled out a handgun. I was expecting to see some kind of high tech automatic, but instead he pulled out a 6 shot Ruger SP 101 in a small holster. I knew it was a Ruger, because I owned one just like it, that used to be Nana's. And my bet was that Hank had one for the same reason Nana did, she didn't want to have to remember to rack the slide to shoot. If you need to shoot, it's easy to point and pull the trigger, no fancy business. You didn't even need to cock it.

"OK, guys, let me just get my guns out of the truck and I'll stay here with the dogs. Take care and let me know what you find or see over there"

Tate nodded at me and I hurried out to the truck to get my Ruger and just for the heck of it, I grabbed my Winchester 410 out as well. It's the same shotgun my grandfather had, and it's been passed down in the family. I figured with it, I had a pretty good chance of hitting something in the dark, if I needed to shoot. I keep the Winchester in the truck on the rack behind the back seat, it's good for discouraging wild pigs. Cause they can be ornery little cusses, and you never know if they'll charge at you or run away.

It took a few minutes to get the guys squared away and the walkie talkies turned on and squelched. I would be able to hear everything the guys were hearing, but we wanted to stay as silent as possible, so the walkie talkies were on a little used channel.

The men headed out and I went back into the cabin. Tate didn't have electricity there, but he did have the solar panels as he told me and they powered some nice lights. I turned them all off but one, and then went outside to sit on the porch with the dogs. They all seemed to know something was up, because they clustered around me, and peered intently into the dark.

I heard the men for the first few minutes, but the darkness swallowed up any noise they made after a little bit. It was hard sitting and waiting, but I knew it was for the best. Tate knows these woods well, Jay was also used to walking around in our forest, and I had the feeling that Hank could keep up with both men. I could hear the sounds they were making walking through the bush over the walkie talkie I had, and every so often a very low comment was whispered between them. Mostly from Tate in the nature of a caution where a tree or soft spot was coming up.

I was actually starting to doze a little, after all, I'd had very little sleep the night before, and then had a full day, as well as working the extra shift at Fred's. The adrenaline had basically worn off from Tate's phone call, and while the caffeine from the coffee had helped, I was still tired. I'd made myself comfortable on the little bench on the porch. Blue was insisting on sitting close by me and the other dogs had made themselves comfortable in a semi circle around my feet.

Suddenly I heard Jay's voice over the walkie talkie. "Shit, damn it, what the fuck" My eyebrows kinda raised themselves as Jay usually didn't employ that kind of language. And the next thing I heard was all of them talking so I looked in the direction they'd disappeared.

"Hey Elle", I heard him say, "Damn, look, can you take the truck out to the road and wait there? I'm calling the doc, we just found Della out here and she's hurt pretty bad. I don't know if Doc.Freitag knows how to get to the old Mathrey place, but I think she knows the way out to Tates' place."

"OK, I can do that, do you need any other help?"

"I'm calling the guys to come out, and Hank needs to call Lee too, I have a feeling this is something he'll want to know about. But if you can, take the truck out to the turn off, and then lead the ambulance and anyone else over to the Mathrey road. From the looks of it, there's been enough traffic on the driveway that they should be able to drive down here."

"On my way" I said.

"And Elle, make sure you have your gun handy, and Tate says to leave the dogs, but take Blue with you if you don't mind."

I hurried up and closed and braced the door and went out to the truck. I told the other dogs to hold and stay and then called Blue. It didn't take any persuading at all to have him jump in the truck. The other dogs just looked at me as if to say, they knew what to do.

My mind was spinning, I had no idea what was going on, and for them to find Della out there, and badly hurt. I tried to think if I'd even seen her with anyone at Fred's that night, but the only one I had noticed her with was Lee. Then we got busy and I didn't have a chance to keep track of either one.

I wasn't as careful going back down the driveway as when we came, at least this time I had the advantage of being able to use my headlights. I swear that road was rougher in the dark than in the daylight, but then again, in the daylight I could see every hole and steer around them. It seemed like it took forever to get to the main road, but I knew it hadn't taken me more than a couple of minutes.

I called Jay back on the walkie talkie and asked if he needed me to come down or do anything. He told me that they had it under control. It wasn't more than a couple of minutes later, Jay called me and asked me to come on down anyway to the Mathrey's place.

"Do you still have your 'mergency pack in the truck?" He asked, "We need whatever you've got in there, it's too far to hike back to Tates' place to get stuff." He paused for a minute and then continued, "I told Doc Freitag to bring a body bag as well. Della's still alive but there's another girl here who needs some immediate medical attention as well as a dead girl we just found. It's a bloody mess here. I gave Freitag and the guys GPS coordinates, just be careful coming down the road, please." I put the truck in gear and thought over what supplies I had in my 'mergency kit'. It was the one my family liked to tease me about. I'd seen some program on TV when I was a kid about how you could carry just about everything you might need in a large coffee can for an emergency if you were stranded in the snow. For some reason I obsessed about it back then and have since kept a coffee can, the old fashioned metal kind, with a supply of matches, tea, sugar, instant soup and a candle in my truck, although I had to replace the candle on a regular basis, cause they had a bad habit of melting in the heat. I'd not found a good solution to that, yet. When I got older, I put that can into a duffle bag, which I kept in the back with emergency space blankets and a fully tricked out first aid kit. Along with a couple of other things. My family laughed at me, but indulged me when I was younger, even though we did live in the south and snow was more or less a once in a 20 years or so oddity, and it never impinged on us. Now, I keep my 'mergency kit' handy. I just update it from time to time. I've dipped into it a few times over the years, using it to help out hikers who've run out of water, as well as a rudimentary first aid. I never regretted my insistence on having my 'mergency kit' handy. I even had Doc Freitag look it over and added other things she suggested. One of which was a pack of sanitary napkins. She swore by them as a great addition to any first aid kit. And she was right, I had used them on a couple of occasions. If you think about it, they are made to be absorbent. Doc had helped me to refine my 'mergency' kit, I now had just what she deemed necessities.

Chapter 11

I managed to make it down to the turnoff to the Mathrey's in just a few minutes. It wasn't that long, but it took much longer. I was shocked at how well groomed the road was, even though the first 50 feet or so was untouched. After I got in a little ways, I saw someone had used something to smooth out the roadway. We don't have dirt roads here; we have sand, and you need to go over it every so often with some kind of grader or put down lime rock to solidify the surface. If you don't, you get big pits where the vegetation that holds the sand together just wears away. And you can get stuck fairly quickly when it's just loose sand. I know about that one, so I now drive a truck with 4-wheel drive. Trust me, it helps when you get bogged down. So my truck wasn't bouncing all over the place which augered well for the ambulance coming out from town.

I came to a stop as soon as my headlights saw the guys. Hank was down on his knees beside a body that was lying on the dirt. Della was leaning against Jay, and Tate stood, looking down at something else.

As soon as I opened the door to step out, Della thrust herself off of Jay and stumbled towards me. She was missing one of her breakneck heels, and her top had been torn down from the shoulder. I could see her shorts had been ripped as well. I got all of that in a flash before she got to me. As she got up to me, she started to fall, and I grabbed her. I could barely hold onto her, and in fact, ended up sitting on my butt with her in my lap. Jay came over, helped Della up, and then gave me a hand to pull myself up with. I looked at Jay, and he shook his head.

"Della," he said, in a gentle, soothing tone of voice, "Elle will help you; just let her get her stuff out of the truck. Della, do you understand me?"

He then took her arm and gently led her over to the back of the truck.

"Get your 'mergency kit out, I think Della needs a blanket, she's cold." In a soft voice, he continued, the kind of tone you use with an injured animal who can't understand the words, just the tone, "I think she needs to sit down. Don't you, Della?"

I just nodded at Jay over her head.

"Come on, Della, come over to the seat here, OK? I've got a nice blanket here we can wrap around you." I said, taking her by the shoulders and leading her to the truck. I continued in the same tone of voice that Jay used. I don't think she understood anything we were saying but was responding to the tones in our voices. From what I could see, she looked pretty rough.

Not only had her clothes been torn, but she had a massive bruise on her cheek, and I was betting she would be sporting two black eyes by morning from the size of the bruise. Her lip was cut and oozing blood, and her arms were scratched up as well. As I helped her into the truck, I took off her remaining sandal put it on the floor, and noticed she had several gashes and scratches on her legs, as well as a severely swollen ankle. I grabbed the space blanket I keep in my 'mergency kit', unwrapped it, and shook it out before folding it around her. She was shivering so hard by this time that her teeth were chattering. I grabbed a bottle of water and held it to her mouth to see if she wanted a drink, but she wasn't even tracking enough to open her mouth. She grabbed my hand as I put the bottle away and wouldn't let go. Her mouth opened and closed a couple of times, and I caught a whiff of something unpleasant. She'd voided herself, and I was just glad that the blanket I had wrapped around her was keeping it off my truck's seat. Not nice of me, I know, but I didn't want to clean feces off the seat.

I just held onto her hand and let her feel my touch. I've never seen someone in such deep shock, to the point that they can't even talk.

Della was almost catatonic. I had no idea what to do for her, other than to sit there and hold onto her hand. I looked over at Jay for advice and he just shook his head and shrugged his shoulders, so I guessed he wasn't too sure what to do either.

Hank and Tate were over to the side of the truck, huddled together and talking about something. I could barely distinguish their bodies, but it looked like Tate was explaining or pointing to something in the bush behind us. Then Hank walked over to me.

"Hey Elle, Jay said you had some first aid supplies here? I don't know how much good we can do until we get the doctor out here. This other girl was bleeding pretty bad, and Tate managed to put a compress on her leg, but I don't know." He shook his head and continued. "How long will it take for the Doc to get out here?

"It took us almost 40 minutes to get to the turnoff to Tate's place, but the driveway down to Mathrey's is a little closer, so you can shave 10 minutes off? They won't have to shut the lights off and crawl down Tate's driveway, either. The kit is in the back here. I got a blanket out for Della, but there are also some gauze compresses, there's also some sanitary pads you can use for the other girl. See if there is anything else there you can use."

I finally managed to free my hand from Della and reached into the truck to shut it off and turn off the lights, but when I did, Della let out a whimper and started to panic again. So, I turned the truck back on and the lights and Della calmed down.

Jay approached me and started filling me in as I sat with Della.

"We've got some mess out here. There's a girl over on the porch there who's barely alive. Hank and Tate did what they could. Tate said she had a bad cut on her leg and was bleeding out, so he put a pad on it but said that he didn't want to do anything else until Doc got out here. We also found another girl behind the cabin; she looked like she was running away when she tripped. I brought her out front before I realized she was dead. I can't tell more than that until I get some more lights out here. I tell you, Elle, I've never seen anything like this. I don't want to go exploring more in the dark; if there's any kind of evidence or trail, we'll just muck it up."

"Do you know who the girl is on the porch?" I asked. Della reached out again and grabbed my hand. It was as if she needed to feel someone alive. She whimpered and said something, but I couldn't determine what she said. She then cleared her throat, let go of my hand, and motioned towards the water bottle. I handed it to her, and she tried to get it up to her mouth, but she was shaking so badly that no matter how she tried, she couldn't keep the bottle steady enough to take a drink, so I held the bottle for her, and she took a couple of sips.

Jay just shook his head.

"I have no idea; I want to wait til Doc gets out here and the guys as well. I told them to bring out some lights, and Hank called Lee to tell him what else we needed. I don't think much is going to get done until morning." He motioned toward Della and continued, "Can you tell us what happened out here, Della?"

Della whimpered again and turned her head into my shoulder, so I was forced to put my arm around her. She was shaking so hard it was hard to keep a grip on her.

Jay just looked at me and asked if I could continue to sit there with Della. And to let him know if she said anything. I just nodded and crooned to her, just like I used to do for Eric when he woke up from a bad dream. It soothed him then and seemed to be soothing Della now.

Jay walked away, and I sat with Della, waiting for the ambulance and the rest of our little police force to come out. At this moment, I wanted nothing more than to go home and leave what looked to be a horrible nightmare behind.

Della finally stopped shaking and started talking, whispering, under her breath. I couldn't make out the words, but she kept repeating what sounded like the same phrase, and finally, her voice got louder.

"Baddelback, baddel back, baddelback," Repeating three times, stopping to get her breath and then repeating it. Repeating it so fast it was hard to make it out, then she slowed down, and the words separated a little, and I could make it out.

"Bad del back." repeated over and over.

I looked over at where Jay was standing with the other guys, and luckily, he looked back at me, and I motioned him over. Della was still repeating those three words and stopping in between. Jay crouched in front of her and asked her what she meant, but she kept repeating the same phrase. And then she just collapsed in on herself again. I didn't think we would get any more out of her for a while.

"Elle, when the doc gets here, have her take some blood from Della; I want her to run a test on her blood and see if there's anything in there that shouldn't be." Jay said, then got up and walked over to Hank and Tate again.

Just then Blue started making a low crooning sound and, jumped out of the truck and walked back the way we'd come. I called to him, but he ignored me, looking intently up the road. I could see him in the faint glow of the tail lights. It took a couple of minutes, but then I could hear what he'd heard, the sirens. I could make out the shrillness of the police siren and the whompa sound of the ambulance. It didn't take more than another couple of minutes, and we could see the flashing red and blue lights of both the police and ambulance. As they got closer, it looked like we had the entire police department coming down the road.

And it was the complete department.

All three cars.

As they got closer, they tried to jockey for position and get ahead of the ambulance, but they didn't count on Doc Freitag. I'm not sure what she was in a former life, but she can out drive just about anyone in this life. By the time they all stopped, Jay was right there, ready to talk to the boys, but Doc got there first. I could hear her blistering their ears with some rather choice comments, and then I noticed that she had Bobby with her. He usually drives the ambulance on the way back from any accident and works as an EMT as well. Doc likes to drive herself when she's called out, though.

Jay stood back for a minute while she finished scolding them for their limited driving abilities and then went over to talk to Doc first. He motioned to me and then over to the porch of the cabin. And while Doc walked over to me, he gathered the rest of his police force together and talked with them.

Doc Freitag crouched down and very gently took Della's hand in hers and spoke with her, but Della was beyond listening and, in fact, was so limp that it was easy for Doc to pull her arm towards her and draw some blood.

"Can you sit with her for a few more minutes? I want to go look at the other girl; from what Jay said, she's badly hurt." She continued, "I'll take care of her first, then I'll be back".

I watched her walk across the yard, winding her way past the cars and onto the porch. She yelled back at Bobby to get something out of the ambulance and started ministering to the girl. During the time she'd been drawing the blood from Della, someone had put up some lights so she was able to see what she was doing.

In the meantime, I was getting somewhat amused at the Keystone Kops antics in the yard. And it wasn't a big yard either. I'd pulled in towards one side of it, and the ambulance was to my right and forward, and the three police cars were all pulled in every which way they could.

It didn't take long for Jay to go over and talk to the guys, and the next thing I saw was the rest of the department getting into two of the cars and getting into each other's way as they tried to leave. Between my bone-deep tiredness and my semi-warped sense of humor, the situation was getting the best of me, and I started to laugh. And then I saw Doc pull something over the body on the porch and the laugh died. I knew that whoever was there was dead.

Blue came over and nosed his head under my arm, and I reached down and petted him with my free hand. He seemed to need some comfort as well. He snuggled into the one side of me, and Della leaned on my other side. I couldn't have moved if I'd tried, I was pinned in place.

I watched as Doc came down the steps, walked over to Jay, and spoke with him, and I could see on both of them that it wasn't good news. Hank had been standing over to one side, talking to someone on the phone, and Tate, well, he'd disappeared. Or at least I couldn't see him.

I just sat in the truck with Della, waiting.

As I was straining my eyes trying to see into the dark beyond the headlights and the stand lights that Jay's people had put up, Blue suddenly let out a bay and tore off into the woods, which got everyone's attention.

Jay and Hank were over by the woods within seconds, and the next thing I could see was Tate stumbling out, supported by Jay on one side and Hank on the other. Doc Freitag ran over to them, and by her gestures, she was telling them to bring him over to the ambulance. I was far enough away that I couldn't hear them, but I could see by their arm movements that an intense discussion was underway. Then, Blue came limping out of the woods with something in his mouth and that stopped the arguing. I wanted to see what was happening, but Della still had hold of my hand and wasn't letting go. I tried to pull away, but she just whimpered and leaned in further, so I figured I was there until whenever or whatever happened next.

Blue dropped whatever it was in front of Tate and sat down; I could see his satisfaction with himself from where I was sitting. Tate patted him on the head and leaned down to pick up the object. When he did, the light hit it, and I could see it was a handgun in a holster. I was antsy sitting there with Della, but she wasn't allowing me to budge, and I wanted to find out what was happening.

It took a few more minutes, but then Jay came over and filled me in while Doc looked Tate over.

"I tell you Elle, this is a fucking mess out here," Jay said vehemently. "I don't know what is going on, but it's bad."

I could tell Jay was really upset; he usually likes to use a more colorful turn of phrase, and for him to use what he called 'common language' meant he was agitated.

"I need to talk to Della and find out what she saw, who she was with, and what happened out here." He put his hand up to his head, ran it through his hair, and continued. "I guess you could see that the girl on the porch is dead. She was unconscious when we found her, and I think she was gone before we even got her up there. Then, with Della coming out at me, Tate getting attacked, and the dog bringing out a gun. It's a bloody mess. And I'm going to be just as glad to hand this all over to Hank and Lee and whoever they bring in."

He motioned towards Della and continued, "I want to get Della into town, and see what Doc can get out of her, then I want you to go home and get some rest. I'll call Suzanne and tell her that I'm here until I can leave, which I'm hoping won't be too long."

He reached over me and stroked his hand over Della's hair once, then walked away.

I waited with Della until Doc and Bobby came over and pried her off of me. I offered to go with Doc, but she told me to go home; they could take care of Della. I waited while they loaded her into the ambulance, with Bobby driving this time, and then walked over to Jay and Hank. Doc had looked at Tate and told him to see her in the morning if he needed any help, but he'd waved her off and wasn't in the mood to be taken care of. I wanted to look around a little now that I didn't have Della hanging onto me. And I also wanted to be filled in a little about what was happening.

My mind was whirling around with everything I'd seen tonight, not the least of which was Della being hurt, but also the groomed road into Mathrey's place. And from what I could see from the lights they'd mounted around, it looked like someone had been out there, taking care of the place.

Which was odd in itself. The Mathreys had been a big-deal family around here for a couple of generations, but with the majority of the family in prison, the homestead had gone to ruin. The younger generation had turned to running drugs and guns and had eventually made some pretty stupid mistakes, thinking they were protected somehow. Still, most of them had ended up arrested and were now serving long sentences. I had yet to hear of any of them coming back to the area, but then again, the family home was far enough from town and hidden so well, that no one would have been able to see any activity there anyways.

Chapter 12

I guess it takes a while to round up enough FSIU people to come out to a crime scene in the middle of the night because, by the time I left, a good hour after Doc and Bobby had gone, there was still no one at the Mathrey's but Jay, Hank, and Tate. Jay had sent the boys back to town in two of the police cars, leaving him one at the scene. Having all three of our police cars there was a little excessive. I was so far beyond tired at this point that I was starting to get sick to my stomach and couldn't wait to get home and get some sleep.

I managed to make it home safely and put Scat out while I brewed a cup of tea. Although the tea went to waste as, just the act of making it drained the last of my energy away. I brought Scat back in and collapsed onto the bed, barely getting my shoes off. I don't think I'd ever been so tired, not even when Eric was a baby. At least back then, I napped when he napped.

I managed to get 6 hours of sleep before the phone rang and woke me up, but I couldn't get to the phone before whoever it was hung up. I knew it wasn't one of my family or friends since the ringtone, Jingle Bells, was my default ring. I lay there for a little while, trying to fall back asleep, but I started thinking about the phrase Della had been muttering. She'd been saying baddelback, which made no sense, but then she started separating the words a little, and it sounded like she was saying bad del's back. I had no idea who or what she was talking about. The only Del I knew was Delbert Hawkes, and I don't think she was talking about him at all.

Letting the phrase run through my mind, sent me off to sleep again, and this time round I dreamed of being chased in the woods, someone shouting at me, seeing lights, and in fact ended up waking to the fact that someone was shouting my name and banging on my front door.

I tried to ignore it, but whoever was out there was persistent to the point that Scat started growling. She was generally quiet unless a bear was outside, but the banging and shouting was starting to annoy her as well as me.

I managed to lurch my way out of bed and shouted at the door to hold on a cotton-picking second; I would be there in a minute. I took the time to hit the bathroom on the way as my bladder was letting me know it needed attention before I answered the door.

By the time I got to the door, I was steaming a little. No one I knew was that rude or persistent, and if it had been one of my family they would have just opened it with one of their keys and come on in. Looking through the window onto the little enclosed porch, I could see it was Lee. I still hadn't talked to him since he'd arrived in town and I really didn't want to see him right now. I'd just crawled out of bed, and I'm sure I looked it.

As I opened the door, he had his FSIU badge out and was showing it so that I knew he was there on official business.

"Lee". I acknowledged his presence.

"I need to speak with you about what happened last night out in the woods," Lee said, "I've got statements from Jay, and Hank is handling the interview with Tate. I needed to find out what you know as well. We've got three murders out there, and there may be more."

I just nodded and stood aside so he could come in the door. Scat was sitting behind me; she's not the bravest of dogs on a good day, but she sensed something was up and was sticking close.

"You're going to need to wait a few minutes; I need some coffee before we talk."

With that, I walked down the hallway to the kitchen and started to put some coffee on to brew. I could feel Lee behind me, and I sensed he was curious. It had been over 20 years since he'd been in this house, and I was living with Nana at the time. I'd changed up quite a few things, mostly getting rid of some clutter and painting the walls. I could hear Scat's toenails on the kitchen tile floor as she made her way over to her bed.

"What do you take in your coffee? " I asked, " I don't have any creamer or fake sugar, so you're stuck with milk and real sugar."

I turned to the cupboard to pull out a couple of mugs and the sugar. As I set them on the little scrubbed deal table, I noticed that Lee wasn't as pulled together as I thought. He looked tired, and there was definite beard stubble on his face. His shirt was wrinkled and looked as if he'd slept in it.

"While the coffee is brewing, I'm just going to go and change and brush my hair. Why don't you sit down? I'll be right back."

I felt at a disadvantage by being woken up so abruptly and having Lee insist on coming in right then. I'd pulled on my emergency robe to answer the door. I usually didn't bother with robes. When Eric was home, I pulled my sweats on in the morning. I had gotten in the habit of making sure I was dressed before coming out of my bedroom cause I never knew just how many boys would be asleep in the living room. Eric had a habit of letting his friends crash at our house when it got dicey at their places. And we won't talk about when I found out that his best friend Gary had been living with us for almost three months before I figured it out. Eric would sneak him in at night and let him out first thing in the morning before I got up. Gary had a marginal home life, and he'd managed to get kicked out of the house with nowhere to go their senior year. I was already used to Gary staying over most weekends, but during the week, they had an elaborate timetable of sneaking Gary in and out so I wouldn't twig onto it. Once I found out, I just let it be official: Gary lived with us until graduation. And my grocery bill didn't even go up that much, as I'd been feeding Gary for months at this point. He was now off at college with Eric.

I didn't hurry up with dressing myself; I even toyed with the idea of maybe taking a quick shower but decided that I wasn't comfortable enough to do it with Lee in the kitchen. But I could and did brush my teeth even though it would make the coffee taste funny. Just something about having a freshly washed face, and clean breath can do wonders.

By the time I got back to the kitchen and Lee, the coffee was finished brewing, and he'd even poured me a cup. Which just happened to be at drinking temperature.

As I picked up the cup, I noticed that he was looking around the kitchen and paying particular attention to our brag wall. The wall where I put all the pictures of Eric with any and all new accomplishments. I loved looking at it from time to time. I'd captured small moments and major triumphs in his life there. His face when he navigated the 'adult' toilet for the first time, the sloppy and huge bows on his shoes when he'd finally learned how to tie them up. His first fish, first day of school, and many other firsts. Nana had gotten me started on taking the pictures; she said that they would keep me from losing it when he became a teenager and hormones took over his brain. All I would have to do was look at the pictures of him, and I would forgive him for everything. And she was right.

With his cup in hand, Lee motioned to the wall and asked, "Who is he?"

"My son Eric. He's in college right now trying to figure out what he wants to do with his life."

Lee got a funny look when I said that, and kept looking from me to the pictures of Eric. I wondered, would he be able to see the resemblance between them at the same age? But he didn't, as the next words out of his mouth was a question about Tate and why Tate would call me and not anyone else.

"Tate called me because my number was the first one on the speed dial, simple as that" I replied to his irritable question. "And as to why he wanted a phone, Tate told me he'd been seeing stuff out in the forest and didn't like what he saw."

I stopped, took a long swallow of my coffee, and then set the cup on the counter. I glanced over at the little table by the window and realized that my latest letter to Eric was sitting there. I'd gotten in the habit of writing letters to Eric when he was just a baby, talking about whatever new thing he'd learned that week or new adventure he'd had. In time, it had become my journal. I don't think Eric had ever read any of the letters, but I liked the idea that maybe sometime in the future, I could hand them over to him, and he might treasure them a little.

I'd written Eric two letters this week, one about finding the body of that girl and another about Lee coming to town and telling him that Lee was his bio dad. I couldn't remember if I'd put either letter away yet or if both were sitting there.

"What do you need, Lee?" I asked, "I haven't had a lot of sleep the past couple of days and I'd like to go back to bed and see if I can nap a little before I have to go to work later on."

Lee just looked at me, and very coldly said, "I need you to make yourself available for questions later today. There is something funny going on around here."

I just looked at him over my cup and replied, "There's always something funny happening around here. And I'll be here or over at Mom and Dad's place if you need me to answer any questions. Or you could just call Jay and have him bring me in."

Just the way Lee kept looking at me put my back up; his questions were almost antagonistic.

"I'd like to know what's going on myself. Finding that poor girl half-eaten wasn't exactly my idea of a good time in the old town. Having Tate start talking about weird stuff happening in the forest is not good either. You'd almost think the Mathrey's were back and up to their old tricks."

I got up from my chair and pointed towards the door, "You can leave any time you like; I'm going back to bed for a while. I'm on the schedule for tonight, and Fred's will probably be pretty busy."

Lee got up and walked towards the door, and just before opening it, paused as if to say something, but ended up shaking his head, opening the door, and walking out.

Scat got up from her bed, came over to me, and rested her head against my side. She didn't like the feelings in the room either. She was pretty darn sensitive to my feelings and stuck close by whenever she could.

Chapter 13

I was so tired from working at Fred's two nights in a row and running out to Tate's in the middle of the night that I had forgotten I didn't have to work tonight.

I'd managed to get a few more hours of sleep and had woken up just in time to grab a quick shower before heading into Fred's. I didn't even take the time to dry my hair; I just pulled it back into a wet braid.

I arrived with just minutes to spare before my shift started, and then discovered I wasn't even on the schedule, since I'd picked up the shift the night before. I decided to forgive myself for forgetting. It had been a crazy few days. I'd found the remains of that poor girl, then with Lee coming to town, Tate calling me in the middle of the night, it was no wonder I'd gotten confused. I decided that since I didn't have to work after all, I'd visit Mom and Dad.

I stopped on the way out to pick up Skat, since she loved visiting my parents. I don't think we even thought about leaving our animals home, they were as much a part of the family as the kids. And while it may have gotten a little rowdy from time to time, everyone got along.

As I drove up to the house, I saw Skat outside, pacing back and forth in front of the house. I knew I'd left her in the house, so for her to be outside was scary.

As soon as I pulled the truck into my driveway, Skat ran over to me, yipping, whimpering, and crying. I could see blood on her face, and dripping down onto her white chest.

I fell out of the truck; I was in such a hurry to check

her out and landed ended up landing on my knees, but I got right up and ran over to her. As I passed my hands over her, I could see a shallow cut on her side, but that appeared to be the only injury. The cut had stopped bleeding, it was just oozy, but she had a lot of blood on her muzzle and it was fresh, and still dripping a little.

It wasn't hers.

Skat was shaking hard and still whimpering as if she was trying to tell me a story about what happened out here. She didn't even try to lick her mouth, and I didn't like that.

I grabbed my phone and called Jay and told him something was wrong. I wouldn't go and investigate without Jay or someone from the Sheriff's department there. All I could do was hold Skat, talk to her, and see if I could calm her down.

When she stopped trembling and whimpering so much, I heard sirens and knew Jay or one of his deputies was almost here.

I hugged Skat closer and told her Uncle Jay was almost here and not to worry. I knew she didn't understand the words, but she knew Jay's name, and her tail started to wag a little.

I wanted to wipe the blood off of her face, but I also wanted Jay to see it first. My thought was that she'd bitten someone, and maybe the blood could be used to check either DNA or type or... I guess I watch too many crime shows.

By the time the police cruiser fishtailed into the driveway, Skat was almost calm. I had her sit while I got a cloth out of my truck, and waited for the driver of the police car to get out. I was so thankful it was Jay, I knew my brother could see what was going on without needing to go into details.

As he approached, I could see the shock on his face; my usually pristine-looking white dog looked like a bloody mess at first sight.

"Jay, I need to wipe off her face, but I wanted you to see it before I do; the blood isn't hers."

"Hold on a second before you wipe it off; I want to take a picture." Jay got out the camera, and Skat sat nicely for him; she'd always been a bit of a ham when it came to having her picture taken, so even though she was still trembling a little, she waited until she heard the click of the shutter, and then came over to him.

I had a cloth ready to wipe, but before I could get to her, Jay had pulled on a pair of gloves and held out his hand for the cloth. He wiped her face, then checked out the shallow cut on her side. I watched as he put the fabric into a Ziploc bag he'd pulled out of his pocket.

"I don't like this, Elle," he said, " I need you to stay here with Skat while I check out the house. I'm calling Lee, with Della being attacked last night and now Skat being hurt. I don't think it's all a coincidence."

I was just as happy to stay put and wait with Skat. I returned to my truck and reached under the seat for my Ruger. It used to belong to Nana, but she had given it to me years before. She wasn't worried about running into any animals out in the woods, but as she put it, you never can tell what a two-legged snake will do. Years ago, we still had a few Mathreys running around. Every town has that one family; they almost toe the line legally but have their fingers in just about every shady enterprise in the town or county in our case. I'd had the gun out the other day so I knew it was still loaded.

I watched as Jay walked around the back of the house, his gun drawn and held down by his side. He was being cautious in case someone was still around.

As I was waiting for him to come back, a second police cruiser came skidding onto my driveway and stopped just inches from the back bumper of Jay's car. I watched as Bill Bowers unfolded himself from behind the wheel, stepped out, and stretched. Bill is 6' 7" and a former football player who also works as a part-time deputy when needed. He makes most vehicles look small. Then the passenger door opened, and a man I'd never seen before stepped out. I don't think I'd seen such a contrast between two men. Bill, on the one hand, was well over six feet tall, and this man might have reached 5 feet on a good day. He was also dressed just a little too fancy to be from our neck of the woods; in fact, he reminded me of a riverboat gambler, or at least how I would have pictured one.

Jay came out from behind the house just then, with his gun holstered, and came over to Bill, said something to him, and then walked over to me.

"Skat's earned a steak dinner today; someone broke the window by the kitchen table and tried to get in. It looks like Skat jumped out the window, scraped her side on some glass, but she also managed to nail whoever broke in.

There was a trail of blood leading into the woods." He paused and then continued. "I found a pocket from a pair of pants with blood on it, and as soon as Lee and Del get here, we'll go ahead and see what else we can find."

He bent down, ruffled Skat's ears a little, and told her she was a good dog. She just wagged her tail and looked satisfied with herself.

"I'd like you to stay out here with Skat for a little longer. Then you can go in and see what's what."

He then walked back over to Bill and the other guy, and I just sat and hugged Skat. My scaredey cat dog had defended her house, I was amazed. This was the dog who would hide behind me when I answered the door. It shows you don't know an animal all the way.

Lee had driven up while I was talking with Jay, and he stopped to speak with Bill and the stranger. Then Jay walked over to them, and it looked like they were having quite a discussion. They turned and looked at me a couple of times. Jay waved at me to come and join them, so I hopped down from the truck and with Skat pasted to my side we walked over to them. I had a feeling she would be sticking as close as glue to me for a while.

The guys were all talking animatedly to each other as I walked over to them and they barely acknowledged my presence. It seemed as if Lee and the stranger were disagreeing on something, but then I heard Lee say "Yes sir, I know, but..." and the stranger replied with, "I've got the documentation, and you need to look at it, now."

With that, the little man stepped over to me and introduced himself as Mr. Pike, and added that he was with the bureau and that Lee and Jay needed to look at some files he'd brought with him, and that he would appreciate it if I would come into the office as well.

I thought it wasn't a request but more along the lines of an order. I looked over at Jay and told him I would come in as soon as I had taken care of Skat and that she would also be coming in. Mr. Pike just nodded and then turned away to Bill and asked to be taken back to town. I watched in some bemusement as Bill turned away and got in the car.

As soon as they drove off, Jay, Lee, and I walked over to my front door, and Jay opened it with my key. I waited while they went into the house, following as soon as Jay shouted an all-clear.

When I walked into the hall by the kitchen, I could immediately see where someone had tried to break in. There was window glass scattered over the table and onto the floor, but there was also some blood. Some of the glass on the side of the window pane had white hairs caught on it and I assumed that was where Skat had jumped out and cut herself. But there was also blood by the latch on the outside door that had smeared and dripped a little.

"Elle, I need you to stay out of here; I want to get some blood samples and see if we might have gotten lucky enough to get a fingerprint." Jay added, "Take care of Skat, and I'll board up this window as soon as we've got what we need. And then we're heading into town."

After I'd washed out the shallow cut on Skat's side, I could see where it was more of a scrape, but it still looked sore. I swiped some antibiotic cream on it, but didn't bandage it. Then I put my attention to her face; I wanted all that blood off of her muzzle; it just didn't go with her gentle personality. I can't say she liked me repeatedly wiping a warm washcloth over her face, but she submitted.

After we finished, I took her outside and waited for Jay and Lee to put a board on the window. As I assumed, Skat stayed glued to my side and didn't want to venture far from me.

Chapter 14

After the parade of cars left to go back to town, I swept up the broken window glass in the kitchen and took stock of what I needed to do. The glass in the window would have to wait to be replaced until the next day when hardware stores would be open. I decided to go ahead and head into town to see why Mr. Pike wanted me to see the papers, and then I was heading over to visit with Mom and Dad. I figured they'd probably already heard about the attempted break-in, and I wanted to reassure them that we were OK.

I'd gotten some blood on me when I was cleaning Skat's face off and decided to go and shower again, as well as change my clothes. I felt dirty and violated. Even though the person hadn't even gotten into the house, thanks to Skat.

I'd handed her one of her special chewy treats, figuring it would help her to concentrate on something other than her side, but she wouldn't touch it and insisted on coming into the bathroom with me. My not-so-brave dog was back in character.

After the shower, I checked my phone and saw I'd missed a couple of calls, but both numbers were unknown, and there were no messages. I decided to note the time of the calls. I figured it wouldn't hurt.

By the time I'd gotten my hair dried and pulled back into a ponytail, Skat had settled down and was busy chewing her treat, but when I picked up my keys and asked if she'd like to go for a car ride, she jumped right up and came to me, leaving what was left of her treat behind. I grabbed my duffle bag on the way out; I'd packed it right after my shower. I knew I could stay with Mom and Dad, but I wanted a change or two of clothes with me. At the last minute, I went and got my laptop as well.

I felt nervous leaving the house, but I didn't want to stay there alone. I needed to spend some time with my parents, and I knew Skat would welcome the chance to see them and their dogs. As I turned left onto the main road from our driveway, I couldn't help it, I had to stop and look both ways for a couple of minutes to ensure there weren't any vehicles loitering on the side of the road in either direction. And even though nothing was in sight, I felt like I was being watched. But I just put that down to the fact that my home had just been broken into.

I headed towards town, and with every car I passed, I had to look to see if it was a stranger or someone I knew.

I then realized I'd forgotten to ask Jay about Della, if she was doing okay, and since Mr. Pike had also wanted me to stop in the office on my way through town, I stopped in the office on my way to Mom and Dad's.

As I pulled up front, I saw two cars with government license plates parked in front, one of which was in Jay's usual spot and the other in front of the fire hydrant. I laughed a bit to myself because both of them were the typical nondescript car; both were dirty, and it was hard to tell just what color they were, and if it weren't for the government plates on them, they'd fade right into the background.

I parked next door and cracked a couple of windows for Skat; since it was in the shade, she could stay there comfortably and walked down to the office.

I could hear a shouting match out to the sidewalk, and as I pushed open the door to the cop shop, I got an overwhelming feeling of unease and the conversation just stopped, and there was dead silence.

The dapper stranger, Mr. Pike, was standing in the middle of the room, facing Lee and Jay, who looked as if they were a united front. To the side was another man I immediately recognized; he looked like a stereotypical FSIU agent with a black suit, tie, and black shoes. His hair was a comb-over and his face had the flushed fleshy look of someone who imbibed more than regularly. I knew it had been him shouting, as that was the way he'd always communicated. Hugo Foster. Father of Ceb Foster who'd been committed to a mental institution 20 or so years ago for attempting to kill his mother, Hugo's wife.

Jay had that look on his face that he got when he was trying to reason with someone he thought was unreasonable. Lee had a blank look on his face, as if he wasn't even present, only his eyes betraying any emotion.

Hugo glanced my way, barely acknowledging that anyone had even come into the room, and continued to shout.

"There is no way that I'm allowing a pissant little police force like this one to continue to investigate these murders. You boys don't have a chance in hell of finding who's doing this, and the FSIU is taking over. I don't care what the state cops say; we're the ones who should and will be taking this case over. "

By this time, he was shouting even louder, and the spittle was spraying. I was just glad I wasn't anywhere in the range of that. I was wondering if he would stroke out, but by the time he stopped to take a breath, Mr. Pike had started talking.

"I didn't say you weren't capable of doing the investigating, Sheriff, but that the Bureau has a lot of resources that you don't," he said in a hushed voice. "Now, Hugo," turning his body slightly in Hugo's direction, "I know you didn't mean to disparage the sheriff. I would appreciate your sitting back for a minute and getting yourself together."

He turned back to Jay and Lee, "As I was saying before Hugo interrupted me, we have resources that can help you at your request. Mr. Foster has been following a series of murders that have been similar to the young woman's circumstances, and he'd like to be able to come and follow along with you and help you out however he can. I understand that Dr. Hawkes is also in the area, and I'm sure he can also help."

He then walked over to Hugo, stood before him, and said very quietly, "I suggest you pull yourself together, go splash some water on your face and we'll get going".

Hugo, who outweighed the little man by at least a 100 pounds and also towered over him, walked meekly into the back room. I wondered just who he was that he could make Hugo back down like that and quietly walk out of the room. I also noticed Hank wasn't there either, and in fact, no one mentioned him at all. Mr. Pike approached me with his hand extended and introduced himself again.

"I understand you were the one who discovered the young woman who was on the road. Thank you for coming in; I appreciate your time. I had a few questions about the body and what you noticed. Could we sit down over here?" he gestured towards Jay's desk. "I won't take up much of your time. I know you've had a difficult couple of days."

I glanced over at Jay, and he just nodded at me, so I followed Mr. Pike and sat down at the desk.

"You are basically self-employed, I understand? What were you doing on that road? It seems like it's quite some distance from the town." His voice was still quiet but with an undertone of almost menace in it as he asked the questions.

"I collect cuttings from some of the heirloom plants in the woods, mostly from abandoned homesites; I propagate some of them, and others I sell to the nurseries or online." I answered, "I also keep a tally of animals who are killed on the road for a researcher at the university, which is why when I saw the wake of vultures, I figured that a deer had been killed and knew I needed to take a picture for Dr. Weiser. I email him weekly with how many animals I've seen hit by vehicles and where they were. A few of us are out and about a lot who also do the animal tally. I'm not the only one in the area."

"I see, so you weren't someplace new or different then?" he queried.

"I hadn't been on that road for a few weeks, but that's not unusual. I know where many of the old abandoned home sites and cemeteries are, what plants are growing there, and the best time to harvest cuttings or dig up young plants."

"I understand you were called out the other night by a man who lives out of town about something suspicious and that you went with your brother, the sheriff?"

"Tate had called Jay and me about some lights and activity out by him. He's a friend. I'm sorry, I don't understand why you're asking me about him? Does the attack on Della and the other women have anything to do with that young girl I found?"

"Not to my knowledge, but it just seems as if there is a lot of violence here suddenly, and I wanted to know what you might know about it all."

I just shook my head.

"All I know is that I found a murdered girl, called my brother the sheriff to come, and then when Tate, who is a good friend, called about some trouble out by him, I went out there to help. He was also injured that night. "

"Your house was also broken into today, just after you left? What do you know about that?" He continued with the questioning with an almost accusatory note in his voice.

I'd about had enough of the questioning, and I stood up and got ready to leave. "Mr. Pike, I'm tired, I'm scared, my dog was injured trying to protect her home; I've seen more dead people in the past couple of days than in my entire life up til now. I'm heading over to my parents in a few minutes, but I also have a friend in the hospital who was attacked, and I have no idea how she's doing. An old man was also attacked, and I'd like to find out how he's doing as well. Just where are you going with all these questions?"

Mr. Pike just stood up and thanked me for coming in. I looked over at Jay with my eyebrows up in a question, and Jay took that opportunity to ask me to tell Mom to expect two more guests for dinner tonight. And since I knew Mom wasn't planning on having a family dinner, I figured out that Jay had something he wanted to tell us in private, away from the office.

"Gotcha, by the way, how is Della doing? She was really shaken up last night, and I didn't get a chance to ask you about her. What about Tate? Has anyone checked in with him?"

"When I checked with the hospital earlier, they said Della was pretty unresponsive. Her ankle's broken, she's got a dislocated shoulder, and she's not talking to anyone." Jay shook his head, "I'm going to go and see her before dinner and see if she's up to talking at all. I sent Brad out to see Tate, and he got sent back with a rude message, so I think he's okay. He's got all those dogs out there with him as well. I'll check with him later on today. We still have some cleanup to do at the cabin. Listen, Elle, you might want to think about staying at Mom and Dad's tonight; I'd feel a lot better if you weren't alone. I know you've got Skat with you, but she got traumatized pretty bad as well."

"I'll think about it. See you guys later", as I nodded to the FSIU guys and left. For some reason, I didn't want to tell them that I was already planning on staying with my parents for a couple of days; the questioning by Mr. Pike had been borderline accusatory and disturbing to me.

By the time I got out of the truck I was dying of curiosity but knew I could wait. I decided to walk over to Threadbare, Suzanne's shop, and see if Jay had given her a heads-up on dinner or anything. But Suzanne was pretty busy; she had dresses laid over every single surface in the shop, and it looked like she was riding herd on a lot of teenage girls. I managed to catch her eye and just told her that I'd see her later on at Mom's for dinner. She sagged for a second and then grinned and waved. So I got in the truck and drove over to my parents.

Skat started whining just as soon as I turned into Mom and Dad's driveway. As if they had been waiting for her, the dogs came running around the side of the house, skidding to a stop just before they ran into the truck. Skat waited until I opened the door and then pushed past me to jump down and greet her buddies. Both dogs were rescues; Goldie was a little on the dumb as a stump side but had the sweetest personality. She was also a big disappointment as a hunting dog. She'd rather make friends with everyone. On the other hand, the hound dog, Elvis, was almost too smart, but he knew enough to know he had it good here. He was also a big bust as a hunting dog, so he got dumped out in the woods. He didn't like guns or loud noises, hated tramping through squishy mud, and preferred to live a quiet life, not hassling any wildlife.

As I walked around the dogs, Mom came out on the front porch and waved.

"So, how many for dinner, and when are they coming? She asked, "Nana managed to tangle up the windchimes outside, and I couldn't figure it out until I came inside and my cookbook was on the floor.", then she caught me up in her signature mom hug. I just rested inside her arms for a second, soaking up the love, understanding, and mom essence. She continued, "I've got a couple of chickens in the oven, and I could use a hand in the kitchen. Then you can catch me up on what else is going on. Nana yanked your chain, and then it stopped right away, and I knew you were alright; you need to tell me everything." Just then, she noticed Skat's side; the cut was pretty visible against the white on her side. "And what in the world happened to Skat? Go inside right now, and we'll talk." I walked inside slowly, suddenly tired to the core; I hadn't realized how tense I was, but just walking in the door drained the tension.

As I walked down the hall into the kitchen, Dad came out of his office and followed me into the kitchen.

I loved Mom's kitchen; it was bright, cheerful, and welcoming. When they'd built the house, Mom wanted an old farmhouse kitchen. She wanted open shelving where the top cabinets should be and then painted the bottom cabinets white with red doors, which paired well with the fire engine red wall that led upstairs. The Viking stove usually had a pot or two of something cooking on top cause Mom was also fond of making Stone Soup a lot. You know the kind, you throw in bits and pieces of leftovers, fresh herbs or not into a pot and let it simmer for a few hours. And today was no exception; there was a big pot of something simmering away and sending warm and unctuous aromas around the kitchen.

As I stood there and inhaled, my stomach suddenly rumbled with hunger. I hadn't had any food yet, just the coffee that morning with Lee, and suddenly it seemed like ages ago. I could smell the chickens roasting and saw that Mom had her bread bowl on the counter, so I knew we'd also get some of her No-Knead dinner rolls.

Mom came into the kitchen just then and took one look at me, pointed to a chair, and said, "Sit," as she bustled over to the stove and proceeded to dish up some of the simmering soup. "Here, this will take the edge off; dinner won't be ready for another hour."

I had no idea what was in the soup, but it didn't matter; it tasted wonderful. And it was just what I needed. After I'd eaten the soup, she and Dad sat down at the table and waited. So I caught them up with everything that had happened. And bless them, but neither one interrupted me as I was talking; they just let it all spill out.

As I came to the part where I'd found Skat with the blood all over her muzzle, Dad reached across the table and grasped my hand, and when I finished, he came over and gave me a big hug, then walked over to the kitchen door and called the dogs in. As soon as they all came bounding into the kitchen, he walked over to the fridge, removed a piece of leftover steak, cut it into three pieces, one larger than the others, and fed it to the dogs. Skat got the big piece and looked at me in disbelief but didn't question the bounty and hurried up and ate it.

Mom just looked at me, shook her head, and said, "So, how many people are we peeling potatoes for? "

" Jay just told me to tell you there would be a couple extra people for dinner, so seven? But I think you need to know something; I one of the two extras might be Lee."

"The Lee?" Mom questioned.

I nodded my head. I couldn't remember if they'd ever met him. The summer we were in love seemed a lifetime ago now. Dad had a contract in Dubai that summer, so I'd been staying with Nana. None of my family, apart from Nana, had actually met Lee. My feelings for Lee were gone, lost in the mists of single parenthood, scrambling to make a living, raising a son by myself.

"It's okay. It's been so many years, and Lee has no idea Eric is his son. I want to see what kind of man he is before I tell him." I looked into their faces, the concern and love stamped so clearly on both, and continued, "Are you okay with that?"

Mom just nodded, and Dad, well, Dad just said, "If that's what you want, we can do it." Mom and Dad had no idea just how shattered I'd been when Lee had returned my torn-up letters and then had used his mother to tell me to leave him alone. Nana had been my rock then, and by the time Mom and Dad had returned stateside, I was well along in my pregnancy, and all I got from them was unquestioning support.

"Well, if we're going to peel potatoes for that many people, we'd better get going." With that, Mom got up and walked over to the sink.

Dad just stood up and hugged me again, then walked over to the kitchen door and said he was going to see if they had any vegetables that could be picked and used for dinner.

And with that, my world fell back into place again.

Chapter 15

It didn't take long for us to peel the potatoes and get them cooking while Dad brought in some fresh chard from the garden, which we cleaned and chopped up next. Mom also had an acorn squash she'd roasted the day before and decided we could mash that up and serve it alongside the chard as another vegetable.

I helped Mom with the dough for the rolls. I don't have her fine touch with them, but I could and did make them into rolls and got them into a couple of pans so they could rise.

The potatoes were cooked, the chickens had been pulled out of the oven to rest, and the rolls had been put in when Jay walked in with Suzanne, Hank, and Tate.

I think this was the first time Tate had ever been in this house. He'd occasionally accept a dinner invitation from Nana or myself, but he preferred to stay out in his little cabin. When he did come to dinner, he never came empty handed, and today was no exception.

He had a mason jar filled with comb and honey in his hands. Tate could always find the best places for honey, and he'd raid wherever the bees took up, taking just a little from each hive. He pushed it out towards my mother, and she took it from him.

"Thank you so much; this will go a treat with the rolls we're having with dinner." She turned away, put the jar on the counter, and continued, " Jay, you know where the beer and the wine is; please serve Hank and Tate whichever they would like, and as for you pregnant lady," motioning to Suzanne, "I don't know what sounds good to you, but there's tea, lemonade, and milk in the fridge. And dinner is almost ready; we're just waiting on the rolls to come out of the oven." Motioning towards me, she added, " Take some of that comb out and put it into a dish so we can enjoy some fresh honey with our dinner."

Jay walked over to the fridge and pulled out three beers, handed one each to Tate, Hank, and Dad, then motioned to me, and I nodded, so he pulled out another beer, opened it, and handed it to me. I wasn't in the mood for wine tonight; I wanted the bitter hop taste of a beer.

After he'd opened his bottle and taken a long drink, he spoke. "I have no idea what is going on out in the woods, but the FSIU is now on the case, and we're just spectators. Hank here told me that there are going to be a bunch more guys coming in." He sighed and continued, " Lee is heading the investigation; Hugo's here as well, but he's been sidelined, he thought he should be in charge, we seem to be the latest stop for some crazy murderer; they've been tracking him for years, but every time they get close, he stops killing and doesn't leave any evidence behind other than bodies. "

Hank interrupted him then, "He does leave evidence, but it's confusing; the only thing the murders have in common is that young women are involved, and each murder scene is different. It's almost like they're staged to confuse."

"Enough talking about murders. We're getting ready to eat now, and I don't want to hear any grisly stuff over the dinner table." With that, Mom turned to me and told me to take the rolls out of the oven and put them on the table while she went to where the chickens were resting and proceeded to cut them up.

The rest of us followed along, Jay grabbing the potatoes and putting them on the table while motioning to Hank and Tate to sit down; Dad grabbed the rest of the vegetables as Suzanne put the pitcher of lemonade by her place at the table.

Growing up, we always had one rule at the table. No unpleasant subjects. Nana believed you couldn't enjoy a meal if you talked about anything negative. If we failed a test at school, we held it back until after dinner; if the phone rang during dinner, no one answered it. Dinner time was family time, and nothing was allowed to interfere. I did the same with Eric as he was growing up. No school talk unless it was good; dinner time was family time, even if we were just a family of two much of the time. We held to the same rule even when his friends joined us for dinner.

Skat came over and lay by my side as I sat down at the table. She'd laid down on the dog bed in the corner of the kitchen while we were making dinner, leaving it for only a minute to greet Tate before returning to lie down again. I was concerned about her but figured she'd bounce back soon enough.

By the time dinner was over, I was dying to know what was going on. It wasn't like Jay to maneuver a dinner like this, but I knew he had more to share, and I was right.

After we'd tidied up the kitchen, gotten the dishes in the dishwasher, and put the leftovers up, we went into the living room, where Dad lit the fireplace. I helped Mom bring in the coffee and poured each of us a cup, and Suzanne had herb tea.

We were all ready to hear the rest of the story.

Jay started to tell us the back story but then asked Hank if he could fill us in.

Hank took a long drink from his coffee cup and started. "The FSIU is here because I called them. Jay called me when Elle found that first girl; it didn't look like a random kill that just got dumped here, and he wanted my take on it. When Jay and I looked a little closer at where she was dumped and how she was killed, it reminded me of a murder in Oregon I'd heard about. There have also been at least three other killings of young women the past few months, all dumped at the side of the road. The ages of the young women were very similar. So I called a friend over at the FSIU and asked if he could remember anything about it and, if so if he could let me know. When I didn't hear back from him that day, I called him again. He told me he'd looked into it and that it was similar to the one I thought I remembered. I got a call back after I'd talked to him and was told someone was coming out to look at it, who was familiar with the other murders, but I didn't expect to see so many agents coming into town. I was expecting one guy, but ended up with Lee, Hugo Foster, and Mr. Pike. Hugo muscled in on the case. He's not well-liked, but I guess you figured that out. His wife is from this area, and I think he wanted to come back here to show off. When he arrived, he tried to bulldoze Lee off the investigation, and then when Tate called Elle, and we came out to that cabin and found Della and the other girls, Hugo went ballistic. He was ranting and raving, and I guess Lee called his boss, Mr. Pike. Mr. Pike is in charge of most special investigations and assigns agents to work on them. He's a legend in the bureau. Jay told me the cabin where you found Della and the other girls, belongs to Hugo's wife's family and filled me in on them. They weren't all nice, upstanding citizens. At least Hugo's wife's grandfather was a sketchy character."

Tate interrupted him at that point and said, "Sketchy? That ain't the right word for him. He was a thief and a scoundrel. He and his wife, Viv, had four kids who lived and several stillborn. She hardly came to town, but when she did, you could see the signs of a hard life on her. Their oldest, Ceb Jr., brought Sheriff Mo to town, and he wasn't no better than he needed to be. When Ceb Jr. died in the war, Mo returned to town, ran for sheriff, and he and Onie got hitched. The kids ran wild, figured that their daddy was sheriff, and they didn't have to listen to anyone. Their oldest girl, she's the one who took one look at Hugo and decided he was her ticket out of there. Hugo was in here after a whole bunch of marijuana washed up on the beaches after a hurricane. The FSIU was here investigating the coincidence of so much marijuana washing up on the beaches. I don't think they got, but a little bit of it; the local good for nothings had already found most of the bales and had it hidden away. There was a lot of hard feelings here for a long time. Lots of folks thought that Mo's boys had a hand in all the marijuana sales roundabout. After Ceb and Viv passed on, Mo and Onie took over the cabin but moved into town cause Mo figured he was too far out to do much good as a sheriff. His boys took the cabin over after a while. Both boys ended up in jail, one of them for assaulting a federal officer and the other for having sticky fingers. I've enjoyed the quiet out there since they've been away. Although lately, it ain't been too quiet there. And speaking of quiet and unsettling stuff, I need to get myself back there. With that, he stood up and, bowed to Mom, and continued, "Miss Lilah, thanks for dinner, I appreciate a meal I don't have to fix." He turned to Jay and said, "I'd like a ride back home now if you don't mind. There's been too much going on out there for me to like leaving for too long."

That signaled everyone to stand up and say they

needed to get going. Suzanne walked over to Mom, hugged her, and thanked her for the meal; as she said, with prom coming up, it was beyond hectic in her store, and being able to eat a meal someone else prepared was a blessing.

After everyone else left, I sat in the living room, exhausted. It had been a tense couple of days, and I wanted to sit and think. Skat lay on the floor with the other dogs in a tangle of legs and fur and seemed content just being a dog.

Mom and Dad came in to say good night and went on to bed, but I just sat there, thinking. There had been so much going on the past few days, and I wanted to sit and just vegetate for a little while, but the thoughts kept swirling around.

Who was that girl I'd found, and who were the other women at the cabin? What were they doing there? Why was Della out there? Who brought her and the other women to such a remote place ? What in the world was going on here?

I wish Nana was here; she sometimes knew stuff or could figure it out. And with that thought, I drifted off to sleep.

I don't know how long I was asleep when a godawful racket started outside. Some of the chains Mom had made were rattling and making noise way out of proportion to their size. Skat began to howl, and the other dogs started barking.

I came off of the couch in one move, and I was at the door in just a couple of steps without even realizing how I got there.

Then I saw it.

My truck on fire, blazing away. By the time it registered that my truck was on fire, Dad was behind me, and I could hear him on the phone calmly telling someone that there was a truck fire and that we needed the fire truck out there.

Then, there was dead silence, and all we could hear was the flames crackling and metal popping as the fire consumed my truck. Until the fire reached, my gun and the ammunition started to go off. Dad grabbed me and threw me to the ground, but luckily, the bullets stayed inside the truck, and none hit the house.

I got up slowly after counting the shots; I was just glad I hadn't put the fresh box of bullets in the truck. I don't think I could have counted that high if they all discharged one at a time. My Ruger only has six shots, which was plenty. I'd taken the shotgun out earlier and left it at my house. So I didn't have to think about it in the truck, either.

It didn't take long for the truck to burn itself out; in fact, the fire was just about done by the time the fire department arrived. They got there in time to hit it with some foam from the fire extinguishers, which quelled the last of the flames.

Jay and Hank pulled in just minutes after the fire truck arrived and watched for a minute before coming to the house.

"Are you guys OK?" he asked, "I got the call just as I was dropping Hank off, and we came right here. I'd sure like to know what in the hell is going on. Hank called Lee on the way here and told him about the fire."

I just nodded and hugged myself.

The stench of fire and burning rubber was burning my nose and eyes, but I wanted to see what was left of my truck. Luckily, I'd parked it well down on the driveway, on one of the pads Dad had made on each side of the drive. We'd all smirked about Dad's insistence on the pads. He didn't want us to do the car shuffle whenever one of us needed to leave after a family meal. So, we all had a spot to park and didn't need to inconvenience anyone else by having them move their vehicles if one of us left before anyone else. Because of this, the only casualty was my truck; it was parked far enough away from the house and any other vehicles so that the fire couldn't spread.

My poor truck was just a shell of metal; the fire had been so intense that even the tires had melted, and it was sitting on the rims. There was nothing left of the interior, just the springs on the seat, no upholstery, nothing. It was too hot to approach, but I could look at it.

As I looked a little closer at it, I could see where the cab looked like a dome, as if something inside had exploded upward.

I was numb and sickened at the same time. I didn't need Jay or anyone else to tell me that the fire had been set deliberately.

I was starting to feel as if I had a target on me. First, my house was broken into, and Skat was injured trying to protect it. And now my truck was torched?

My nice, safe little life was starting to unravel.

Jay, Hank, and I returned to the house when the fire department had cleaned up and left. Mom had a pot of coffee going; she'd made periodic forays out to check on us, but for Mom, her way of showing concern was by feeding people or making coffee. Dad had returned to the house earlier and stayed with the dogs otherwise they would have been underfoot and in the way.

We sat at the table, and Skat immediately sat at my feet as if needing comfort.

Before Hank could get started on what he wanted to tell us, the doorbell rang, and Jay got up to answer it, I could hear some low voices, and when he came into the kitchen, following behind him was Lee.

Mom and Dad were as gracious as they always were while Hank introduced Lee to them, and Jay just sent me a look as if to ask if I was OK with it. All I could do was shrug my shoulders.

Lee was there in his official status, and there was nothing I could do to stop him from being there, but I was curious if he would enlighten us. I was still in shock from having my truck torched, but was so glad I wasn't by myself in my house. After Lee accepted a cup of coffee and sat down with us a little of the FSIU sheen had left him.

He started off by thanking Mom for the coffee and then asked if we could all keep a confidence. Hank interrupted him then and told us, "I spoke with Mr. Pike, and he said that SA Cross could feel free to tell us all that he's learned so far about the murder of Angela Harry, who is the woman that you, Elle," motioning to me, "found and he can also tell you about the other murders he's been investigating for the past couple of years." Hank nodded and added, "I hate to say this, but your friend, Del, may be involved. I'll let Lee tell you the rest."

"As far as we can tell, the murders started about 15 years ago." Lee paused for a moment, sipped his coffee, and continued, "I started working with the Bureau after graduation from college, and one of my first assignments was cataloging murders that had occurred across the country. It was make work for me while waiting to be assigned to where they needed me. I was pretty good at it and ended up staying at Chapel Hill for a few more years."

He then continued to tell the rest of the story as far as he knew. Another of his tasks was to look at the statistics of other crimes, Ponzi schemes, and other financial crimes. He'd been heading into his boss's office one day to give a report. He overheard Hugo in there, talking about a murder that his office had been investigating in Oregon and how it was similar to others. He was trying to tie Delbert Hawkes into the murders, as Delbert had been either lecturing or consulting in those areas around the same time. Hugo was trying to get permission to investigate Del. He wasn't having any luck with it, but Lee was also privy to a lot of the paperwork that Hugo generated. Lee had decided to look into the claims on his own. Lee also knew Del was here on leave right now, and while he didn't know the details, he knew Hugo was also here to check Del out.

Which explained why Hugo was in town. I knew a little of Hugo, as I'd met him when Del was a teenager and had just lost his father. I wasn't impressed with him then, and his attitude in the office the other day impressed me even less.

Lee said, " The office told me Del's on medical

leave. With the young woman that Elle just found, Hugo's here to investigate Del for that murder and more."

I had an uncomfortable feeling; Del had confided in me last year and had asked me to keep it quiet about his health. A few years back, he'd been diagnosed with polycystic kidney disease, which had led to his father's death at the age of 44 of an aortic aneurysm, which was a complication of the disease. Del had been undergoing some experimental treatments for it, but they were hard on his body, and he would miss work sometimes. He'd tried to schedule the treatments when he could take leave, but sometimes, the treatments would leave him too sick to work. I'd only found out about it when I ran into him by his place last year and helped him back to his cabin after finding him passed out on a path. He'd told me he'd been trying out some naturopathic remedies that were supposed to help his kidney function. But this particular combination of herbs just made him sicker. He'd also told me that he would schedule lectures near hospitals and medical centers researching and working on kidney diseases. He wanted to keep his illness private.

Lee continued, "I don't think Del is the murderer. Hugo's got something in for Del, and I have no idea why."

Jay interrupted him at that point, "I know why. Del is Hugo's nephew, a constant reminder that his own son is crazy. Ceb used to impersonate Del when they were younger. They looked more like brothers than cousins. Ceb was also convicted of trying to murder his mother and sentenced to 30 years in jail. Hugo and his father-in-law, Chief Falchion, interceded with the judge, and Ceb was sent to Rawcliff Institute for the Criminally Insane instead. He's been there for the past 20 years or so. And I don't think Del would admit to the fact that Hugo is his uncle either."

Jy then added, "Hugo and his sister had a big falling out well before Ceb tried killing his mother. I was out there one day and heard Hugo screaming at Ellen to get the hell out of his house and take that nerdy little twerp with her. Ellen and Del came out of the house and drove away. This was shortly after Del's dad died. I don't think Ellen ever went back there. After her husband died, she became a bit of a recluse and then moved with Del up to Cambridge when he was accepted into MIT when he was 15. They used to come back in the summers when school was out. The property has been in the Hawkes family since the turn of the century. That's where Hank and I ran into Del last week."

    Lee waited a moment to see if Jay had anything else to add, and when he didn't, said, "I wanted to ask if you mind Hank staying on to help you out for a while. I know you asked him in initially, but I don't want to step on any toes. Mr. Pike is sending Hugo back to Chapel Hill, and when he does, I want to be able to concentrate on any new evidence. " He then told us that the blood work had come back on Della, and she had Rohypnol in her system. A lot of it. He added that the problem with Rohypnol was that she probably wouldn't be able to remember much of what happened that night. She was traumatized and was still baseline catatonic. He also said that someone had been staying in the old Mathrey cabin; it looked like it had been cleaned up, and his lab guys were going over it. And with that, he finished with, "But in the meantime, I want to say thank you for the coffee, and I think you all need to get some rest. I know I do." He got up from the table and headed towards the door.

    Skat got up from where she'd been lying at Dad's feet walked over to Lee, and let out a gentle woof at him. He reached down, petted her a little, and continued out of the house. Jay and Hank got up next, and after hugging me, Jay walked over to Mom and Dad and hugged them each as well. "I want you guys to go to bed, and you can talk all this over in the morning. I'm exhausted, and Elle looks like she could fall over any second now. I'll come out tomorrow morning, and we can talk. Come on, Hank, let's get out of here." And with that, he and Hank both left.

Mom looked over at me and said, "Just leave the cups there; we'll take care of them in the morning; we all need some sleep."

I went to let Skat out the door, but she refused to go out, so I just took her up to the guest bedroom. I got inside the room, sat on the bed, and then lay down, and passed out. I didn't undress or even take my shoes off.

I woke up once to go to the bathroom and stepped right onto Skat, who groaned in her sleep but didn't even move. I still had my clothes on, so I hurried up and undressed, then went back to sleep. I woke up again and saw that it was light outside, and I lay there for a minute, trying to figure out where I was. Then I remembered.

It had been such an eventful couple of days that I didn't even want to get out of bed, but because I'd moved, Skat saw I was awake and came over and placed her wet, cold nose right on my leg. She needed to go outside. I could hear voices downstairs and outside as well.

Skat was standing over at the bedroom door, so I opened it and let her go downstairs while I grabbed a change of clothes and headed into the bathroom for a quick shower before I went in search of coffee.

By the time I got into the kitchen, Skat had already

been outside and was back in, looking very pleased with herself. Since I'd heard voices, I knew someone was up and could let her out.

I got myself a cup of coffee and sat down at the table; I wasn't ready to go outside to look at the remains of my truck. And I was even less enthusiastic about contacting the insurance company. My truck was old, but it was paid for and reliable to boot. The thoughts of the whole idea of collecting on the insurance, the hassle of shopping for a new vehicle, and the payments I would have to make were almost more than I could stand.

The door opened as I finished my coffee, and Jay walked in. He walked over to the coffee pot, poured himself a cup and then came and sat down with me. He motioned towards Skat with his head and asked, "How's Skat this morning? She looks rested, and so do you. Feel better? You looked all in last night."

"I do. I didn't even undress; I just fell on the bed and was out. Have you heard how Della's doing? And any news on anything else?"

" Della's still not responding to anything. She'll drink if someone holds up a straw to her mouth but hasn't said a word. Doc said that wasn't uncommon when someone has a traumatic incident like that. They did a rape test on her, but the results were negative; we don't think she had been raped, but someone did beat her. She had bruising up and down her ribs, along with a bruise on her back that's the size and shape of a boot. One of the FSIU agents is sitting beside her in case she comes to and says anything."

"Anyone have any idea what's going on out there? Lee said that the cabin stuff was different from the other murdered girls, but how do they know that?"

"Easy, we found out that Joe Falchion is one of the people staying at the cabin. It seems he was released a few years back, and he decided to come back here and settle down again. He's got a son who's following in his Dad's footsteps; he's already served a couple of short stints in jail. And Buddy was also released a while back as well. "

"Both of them? I remember the stories Nana used to tell about them. Wasn't it Buddy who was suspected of running the marijuana operation for that guy out of Miami? Nana said that was how Hugo came to Berkeys Corner; he was investigating the pot sellers around here. And when Lavinia saw Hugo, she decided he was her ticket out of Dodge. Buddy got caught when he beat up the wrong person."

"Yup, and Joe was sentenced to 20 years for selling stolen property. He was a deputy when they caught him with lots of marine radios and Lorans. The shed in his backyard was full of electronics and computers. That was back when they were pretty pricey. Left Chief Falchion with egg on his face, his son, the deputy, getting caught with stolen goods."

" Wasn't Chief Falchion suspected of covering up a lot of crimes around here as well?"

" Not just the chief, but the Mathreys weren't as good as they could be. It was common knowledge that Ceb Mathrey ran a lot of the illegal stuff around here, and then to get a son-in-law as a police chief meant they could do a lot more without getting their hands dirty. There were a lot of rumors, but every time anyone got close to accusing him, they would somehow decide not to say anything, or they'd leave town and never return. When I was a kid, a black kid was found under the Black Bridge wrapped in chain. Ceb Mathrey comment on that was , "Poor old nigger stole more chain than he could swim with." I don't think anyone investigated it any further. Listen, I need to get back into town. Do you want to look at what's left of your truck? The crime guys from the FSIU will probably come out later on as well, but for now, don't touch anything."

    I got up from the table and walked over to the door. Jay just stood there for a minute and then pulled me into a hug. I stood there enjoying his hug. I needed that. I knew I could count on him to investigate and run interference with the FSIU if needed, nothing like having a big brother who was the local sheriff.

    I wasn't prepared for the sight or the smell of what I saw. My truck was nothing more than a shell of metal. The cab had a dome-shaped bubble on top, as if something had exploded inside and raised the top. The tires were gone, melted, and burned away. None of the glass in the windshield or side windows had survived, and there were holes punched into the driver's door and the passenger door as if someone had fired a gun inside the truck. The lingering acrid odor of burning rubber, cloth, and metal stuck in my nose. You could see where the tires had melted onto the concrete pad and then burned away. The ground beside the pad was churned up and muddy from the water and foam the fire trucks had used to try and quench the flames and then used the hoses to keep everything around from burning up. I just stood in shock for a few minutes. It was more than I could process. Why anyone would torch the truck was beyond my comprehension. After having the house broken into and now the truck, it felt as if there was someone out to get me.

    Why, was the only word that cannoned around in

my brain. Why? Why me? Why my house, my truck?

I must have stood there, staring at the remains of the truck for too long, because I finally came to when a wet, cold nose kept poking my hand. Skat was whimpering a little. She was picking up on my emotions. Whether or not she recognized that the truck she loved to go for rides in was sitting in front of us, she still knew I was upset.

After Skat had gotten my attention, I walked back to the house, my mind churning, turning over ideas and discarding most of them almost right away. I knew I needed to contact my insurance company and see what kind of pittance they would allow me, and then I had to get a new vehicle; whether I rented or bought, I needed reliable wheels.

As I approached the house, Mom came around the corner with a basket. I figured she'd been out gathering eggs from their last three hens. Every spring, she'd buy a dozen chickens, and by the end of the summer, most of them had flown the coop, some involuntarily with the help of one of the hawks in our area.

"Elle, " She said, "Come into the kitchen with me. I want to give you the keys to my car; you'll need something to drive for the next few days."

Which solved my most immediate problem; I wanted to go and get my insurance information from the house so I could call and get that process started. And using Mom's car would solve that immediate problem.

As I walked back into the kitchen, Mom had already put the eggs away and had also put on a fresh pot of coffee. When I sat down at the table, I was shocked. My Ruger was sitting right in the middle of the place mat in front of where I usually sat. I thought I'd lost it when the truck was torched.

"Mom, where did the gun come from?" I asked, "I didn't take it out of the truck last night."

"Dad found it sitting on the front porch this morning, in the chair Nana used to sit in. I thought it was an odd place for you to leave a gun; you're always so careful with them."

"I had it tucked away under the seat in that holster that Dad made me; I thought it had burned up in the truck."

Just then, we looked at each other, and both of us, at the same time, said. "Nana."That was the only explanation that fit. Nana had been looking out for us and me. And since Nana had gifted me the revolver, it made sense that she'd 'retrieve' it from the truck and put it somewhere out of harm's way, although I did notice that the gun wasn't loaded.

After we'd had a cup of coffee and a couple of Mom's Candied Ginger and Lime cookies, I took the keys to Mom's car and prepared to go to my house. Skat was tight beside me as if she wouldn't let me out of sight. I called Jay to let him know I was heading out, as I was nervous about what I might find there and didn't want to be alone there, just in case. He told me everyone was busy, but Bill Bowers would meet me there if that was OK. That was just fine with me. Bill is a former pro football player who retired early, and with a degree in criminology, started writing books and became a best-selling author. He will also help Jay out from time to time, he took a law enforcement class so he could understand a police officer's job a little better for his writing, he said. I knew that Jay deputized him a few years back, and he comes in and helps out from time to time. I also figured that with the FSIU in town, Bill would be hanging out to get some real-life experience with them, and I knew we'd be reading about this in one of his books later on.

As I drove to my house, I prayed it would be intact. The thought that someone could come and torch my truck, sitting outside my parent's house, with all of us inside the house, then who knew what they would do to an unoccupied house that was set in an isolated area.

When Nana had the house built, she was the only one on that road, and it stayed the only house there until a couple of years ago. Our family still owned most of the land surrounding the cabin on both sides of the road. The only exception was a piece about a mile down that had been sold to someone from out of state about 30 years ago. They promptly built a McMansion and then decided we were too far away from civilization. They left the house and attempted to rent it out after trying unsuccessfully to sell it. So far as I knew, there hadn't been any renters there for a long time, years in fact. No one around here wanted to or could afford big city rent. And the house had gradually deteriorated.

While I loved living there, for today, I would have been grateful to have neighbors. Someone could call me if need be, and tell me that something was amiss at my house.

I waited out on the main road for Bill, as I was leery of going down that long driveway alone. I had been there for less than 5 minutes when Bill pulled up behind me. I signaled that I was turning into the driveway, and he flashed his headlights in response.

As I drove down the driveway, I went slow since I was driving my mom's car, and I'm glad I did. You can't see my house from the road; when the road was put in, Nana didn't want to cut down a couple of the big magnolia trees, so she had the driveway wind around them. This meant that not only could you not see the house from the road, but the driveway curved around the trees. And with the shrubs and other vegetation that had filled itself in around the trees, the house was really private.

Just past the first Magnolia tree, a pine tree was lying across the road, which meant I had to come to a complete stop.

That tree hadn't been there yesterday, and I didn't think it had decided to lay down across the road overnight. Sometimes trees fall over, without any encouragement, but they're few and far between.

Bill beeped the horn at me; I could see him in my rear view mirror put a hand up as if to say, stay put. I was going to. I've always wondered about those movies where the 'heroine' goes down in the dark basement after the power goes off and one of her friends disappears. Personally, I'd be out that door like a shot, screaming like a banshee and running away from the house.

Bill started to back his car up and made a come-along motion with his hand, so I put the car in reverse and followed him out to the road. He pulled up, got out of the car, and came towards me. As I got out of the car, suddenly my phone rang with the ringtone I had reserved for Jay, Bob Marley's "Who Shot the Sheriff'. As I answered it, my eyes scanned the brush around us I was nervous. And I noticed that Bill was doing an exorcist impression as well, his head swiveling around as if it were trying to see everything in the front, sides, and back.

"Hey, kiddo," I heard as I answered, "I need you and Bill to come in as soon as you've finished checking out your place."

"We're coming in now; I think Bill was going to call you," I answered, holding up my hand to Bill and putting my hand over the mouthpiece. I mouthed 'Jay' to him. He nodded and stopped for a second. "We're out at my place right now, but we couldn't get down the driveway; a pine tree was lying across it just past the first Magnolia tree."

Bill put his hand out and motioned to the phone, so I told Jay that he wanted to talk to him and handed the phone over.

To say I was a little scared was an understatement. I was a lot scared and nervous. So much had happened over the past few days; it was almost more than I could handle.

I could hear Bill talking to Jay, although he wasn't saying much, but that was the only thing I could hear. Usually, the woods are alive with noise. Birds calling, rustling through the brush, insects buzzing, and the frogs.

But this, this was the breathless stillness just before a storm or when a predator was hunting, when the whole forest becomes silent, with dread or anticipation.

I interrupted Bill and told him we needed to get going, and I guess there was a note in my voice because he just said, "Talk later', clicked off the phone, handed it to me, and started walking back to his car.

I wasted no time getting into my vehicle and,

glancing up into the rearview mirror, saw that Skat was sitting up, looking intently into the woods, and then she started to whine, barely audible, just under her breath. I fumbled a little starting the car; Skat was freaking me out, and I pulled out in a shower of gravel from the roadside, and saw that Bill was right behind me.

I broke the speed limit heading into town; I was terrified. By the time we reached the outskirts of the town, I'd calmed down a lot, but I was still upset. We both pulled up in front of the cop shop, Bill right behind me, but he beat me into the office. I had to get Skat out and on a leash. There was no way I was leaving her in the car. This wasn't her first time coming to the office, and she knew the rules.

Jay met us at the door and motioned towards his office. Skat and I went inside and waited for him. Lee was ensconced on a chair by the desk, as was Hank. With Bill, Skat, and me there as well, the office was a little crowded. Jay came in with a couple of folding chairs, and as he set them up, Hank got up and motioned me toward his chair. I gratefully took it. By the time everyone sat down and shuffled chairs around, the silence in the room was so thick that you could almost see and taste it. Jay's office wasn't that big, but it did have a door on it, and when it was shut behind him, the room got even closer.

I couldn't help but notice the particular man's smell in the air, a combination of sweat, deodorant, and aftershave, mingling and under-laying, a particular acrid smell that seemed to reek of fear. Jay looked at me with some compassion in his eyes, and I braced myself for whatever he was about to say.

"Elle, we found a pair of eyeglasses by your house the other day, and a bandana that I've seen Del wear around here was found by your truck. It's pretty circumstantial, but it looks like he may have been the one who torched your truck. We went out to his place, and he's not there. It looks like he took off in a hurry, but it's hard to tell." He continued, "we've been trying to get hold of Del, but he's not answering his phone, and all the texts have been unanswered."

I interrupted him then and told them all that Del wasn't the one who'd broken into the house or had torched my truck. I couldn't let Del be blamed for any of it. I knew I was breaking a confidence, but they needed to know about Del and his medical condition. I then told them about his illness and that I probably knew where he was right now. Del was in the hospital in Gainesville, undergoing a series of tests to see if he could be a candidate for a kidney transplant. He wanted to be put on the list, which necessitated being admitted and evaluated. He'd been there since last week when he had a bad episode. He'd needed dialysis right away and had elected to stay for the other tests.

Lee just sat there looking at me, reached into his pocket, pulled out his phone, and dialed a number. We could hear his side of the conversation, and it sounded as if he was trying to persuade someone on the other end that he needed Del's file with any medical information in it. He was being stonewalled until he brought up Mr. Pike's name, at which point we heard him say he'd hold for a minute.

We all stayed quiet as Lee talked on the phone. I wanted to hear what was said, as did everyone else. It didn't take but a couple of minutes, and Lee hung up the phone.

"I guess you all heard I was trying to get some

information on Del's medical condition. They couldn't tell me exactly what he's being treated for, but they can confirm he's been on medical leave and has, in fact, been in the hospital in Gainesville for the past 5 days. There is no way he could have been at the cabin the other day or here torching the truck."

Just then, one of Jay's officers knocked on the door and stuck his head in.

"Boss, I think you need to come out here," he said and closed the door. Jay got up from behind his desk, wove his way through our chairs, and went into the main room. Seconds later, he opened the door again and asked all of us to come out.

"We just got a call from Sacred Heart. They got a GSW in there, and the guy's name is Buddy Falchion. He's in surgery right now, but they expect him to live. He says his brother and his nephew are dead. I'm heading over there right now." nodding to Lee and Hank, he added, "you guys come with me." Then, turning to me, he added, "If you want to go check out the tree, take Bill, Brad, and a couple of the FSIU guys with you if that's OK with Lee.", looking over Lee for acknowledgment.

Lee nodded, picked up his phone, and called someone.

"If you guys can wait a little while, I've got a couple of guys on the way here, and they can go with you. The tech team has headed back already, and I have to wait for some guys to come in from Port St. Joe. They should be here within the hour."

It didn't sound like a request but more of an order,

but I didn't mind. I was in no hurry to go back there. The tree lying across the road and the general unreal stillness of the area made me nervous, and having a bunch of armed men with me sounded just the thing. I told them I'd return in a little while and left the office.

Chapter 16

While waiting for the troops to be rounded up, I decided to go and grab some lunch from Give Pizza Chance. I called and talked to Moon, ordered a Calzone to go, and told him I'd be by in a few minutes to pick it up. I wanted to check on Suzanne and see if she had a minute to chat. As I walked up to the store, I looked in the window, and it didn't look like Suzanne had anyone in there. So Skat and I walked in; I knew she didn't mind Skat coming in as we'd visited her there many times. Skat knew where she was allowed to go and, in fact, walked to the back and laid down on a piece of carpeting Suzanne kept by the back office. I heard the toilet flush, and Suzanne came out of the bathroom. She looked pale and shaky, but I recognized the look. Morning/afternoon sickness will do that to you. But even pale, she was still glowing.

"Elle," she exclaimed as she hurried over to me and hugged me, "Jay told me about the truck; I'm so sorry. I'm just glad you weren't out by yourself when it happened. He also told me about the house being broken into and Skat getting hurt."

Skat had gotten up and come over to her, and she also gave her a quick pet.

"How are you doing?"

"I'm OK. I just wanted to pop in for a second and see how you were feeling," I replied, "I'm just waiting for a Calzone, and then Bill, myself, and a couple of FSIU guys are heading out to the house. Bill and I were out there earlier, but a tree was lying across the road, and it gave me the heebies, so we returned to town. Jay'll call you later on, but he's heading over to Sacred Heart; it seems that Buddy

Falchion was shot yesterday, and he said his brother and nephew are dead as well." I just shook my head; there had been so much going on this past week; it was stupefying in its intensity.

"I'm going to go pick up my lunch and see if I can eat it before we have to leave; I just wanted to come in and check on you."

"Before you leave, "Suzanne started, then stopped and continued, "Has Nana been sending you any messages? Jay says she's been around a lot lately, but I haven't heard anything apart from her talking to me that night. "

"She did leave me a present the other night, somehow she got my Ruger out of the truck and left it on the front porch on a chair," I replied, "and she yanked my chain at the house, but nothing else that I can think of offhand. Why?"

"Well, this sounds silly, but I keep finding stuff rearranged here in the shop. I was putting it down to absentmindedness or pregnancy brain because I don't remember doing any of it."

"What are the things that are being rearranged?"

"The high-heeled shoes that I keep here to wear, I've found them tucked away in the back in boxes. I don't remember doing that, and I know I wouldn't."

I started to laugh; I had to. This was a Nana thing. "Yup, Nana's been around. She loved shoes but thought pregnant women should wear shoes that breathe and let their feet swell if needed. She disapproved of high heels for pregnant women."

"Honestly, I've been wearing flats and low heels lately. And sitting as much as possible," she answered. "I guess Nana is around for me as well. I like it."

I hugged her and told her we had to get going. I wanted to eat my Calzone before heading out to the house. I'd not eaten a lot at breakfast, but I was getting hungry and my mouth was watering at the thought of one of Moon's Calzones. I could almost taste it. Skat was up and waiting at the door for me; she knew who Moon was.

As we walked down towards Give Pizza Chance, we were stopped by several people I knew. I wasn't in the mood to talk to anyone, and I knew that if I stopped for more than a couple of seconds, I'd get buttonholed. I just did not want to talk about anything.

There would be gossip; we live in a small town and can't help it. And with the discovery of the bodies and then my truck getting torched, I knew darn well that the local gossip mill was in full swing and grinding away. While I appreciated the concern, I also knew that anyone who could buttonhole me was only looking for a juicy bit of information they could trade with others.

I entered the restaurant, unaccosted and Moon met me at the counter. However, instead of one Calzone, he had a box sitting there. When I raised my brows, Moon told me to take it and go; it was paid for, and not to worry about it. I had to peek inside and saw that he had a double layer of Calzones, inside. So I did. Take the box and leave, that is. Moon also said there was a plain Calzone in there for Skat. And I think she knew it because she put her nose right up to the box and inhaled. If she'd inhaled any harder, the box would have flown open, and those Calzones would have gone straight into her mouth.

I managed to make it back to the cop shop, juggling what was by now a very warm box , nodding and stepping aside a lot, motioning to the box as my excuse for not stopping for a quick chat.

As I opened the door, a cacophony of noise barreled into me. Phones were ringing, voices were raised, and it looked like chaos. Hugo was back and standing right in the middle of it all, with an amazon of a woman standing toe to toe with him, telling him to back off now.

I stepped inside and then took the wall route back to Jay's office; there was no way I was getting involved in whatever was going on.

Just as I got to the door to Jay's office, the woman who'd been toe to toe with Hugo stormed over to me and demanded to know who I was and what I was doing there.

My mouth dropped open, and before I could get a word out, she then said, "And what is a dog doing here? Take that animal outside immediately, and yourself as well."

She continued, "This is a police station, and unless that dog," in an accusatory tone, " is a drug or explosives expert, he has no business being in here."

Just as I opened my mouth to say something, Lee returned to the building and asked what was happening. She then turned to him and said that Mr. Pike had sent her down to help Lee, and she had found Hugo here, ordering the men around, and no one was paying any attention to him or to her. And that this 'woman,' pointing at me, and her dog was trying to sneak into an office.

"Judith", Lee began with a patient, long-suffering note in his voice, " As senior agent here, I'm in charge, not you. Hugo's already been told to leave and not interfere,and he will do so. The men here are all police officers who are employed by the town, and they know what they're doing; they don't need to be told. And the woman you just accosted is the police chief's sister and one of the reasons we're here." Turning to me, I could see a glimpse of the old Lee I used to know as he winked, then he continued, "Judith, this is Elle; she found the first body and was out with Jay and Hank when they found the cabin with the other women. If you come with me, I'll fill you in on the rest." This last said with a fake patience in his voice. I could almost hear his teeth grinding.

I continued into Jay's office with Skat staying right on my heel. She'd gotten scared by that woman, and quite frankly, she scared me as well.

After putting the box of Calzones on the desk, I walked back out and snagged the plates and some napkins that Jay kept by the coffee machine. It had quieted down a lot. Hugo had gone, and Lee had taken Judith into the back into the euphemistically called storage room, which was more or less a glorified closet. Hugo and Judith had, not only been contributing to the noise, but were also a large part of it, and the poor guys trying to answer the phones had to shout over them to be able to talk.

I got my Calzone out of the box, onto a plate, and then took Skat's Calzone out. I knew it was hers; Moon had cut her name into the top, and he'd also put initials on the rest. Mine was the only one without a letter on it. There were an additional five in the box, one with a J, an L, an H, another with a B, and one with just a question mark.

I'd forgotten to get a knife while getting the plates and napkins, so I headed back into the main room, which was much quieter. Bill had just hung up the phone, so I waved at him to come with me and headed back to Jay's office.

His eyes brightened when he walked in; the air was redolent with the gorgeous, rich odors of tomato sauce, cheese and pepperoni. I motioned toward the box and told him that it seemed someone ordered a bunch of Calzones, and I got to deliver them along with mine and Skat's. As he reached into the box for his, I was busy cutting Skat's treat up. Moon makes hers with cheese, sausage, and a little pepperoni, and she was sitting so pretty, waiting patiently, except for the long string of drool coming out of one side of her mouth.

I put her plate on the floor behind Jay's desk, and she hurried up, went over to the plate, and started eating after looking at me for permission. Bill wasn't as polite; he'd grabbed his Calzone and had taken a big bite out of it and was wiping his mouth with his other hand when Jay walked in with Lee, Hank, and Judith.

Jay opened the box, got a Calzone out, and then told Hank and Lee that there was one in the box for each of them.

"I don't know what you like, so I had Moon just make a basic Calzone for you, Judith," Jay said, "please help yourself; the one with the question mark on it is yours. Hank, Lee, I think you can figure out the rest. I figured Elle would be stopping in there for something to eat, so I ordered for everyone. I wanted to go over some things with you, and it seemed we might as well do it and get some lunch."

He then told us what had happened since I'd left that morning. He started with, "The Falchion brothers were both released from prison. Joe's been out for over 15 years, but Buddy's only been out for a few months. He got into trouble for the first couple of years, and his sentence was extended several times. Joe and his son were working in an auto parts store, and when Buddy got out, he moved in with them. Somewhere along the way, they decided to come back here and live. Jay paused to take a bite of his Calzone, chewed, swallowed, and continued, " Buddy said that when they got to the cabin, it looked like someone had broken in and had lived there for a while. They figured if that person came back, they'd just tell him to clear out, and they moved in. There are still some Mathreys in the area, and they weren't concerned about it, figuring it was one of them. A few days ago, Buddy and Joe's son decided to go out and find some female company. They went to the college, picked up a couple of girls in one of the bars, and brought them back to the cabin to party for the weekend." Just then, Judith interrupted Jay with a question. "Were there any drug or BAC tests run on the other two women?" "Doc took some samples, and the lab is running the tests now. It's too soon for the drug results, and the BAC is problematic; too many false positives, but she's doing her best. Della's urine test showed positive for roofies, but they don't think she had anything else in her system."

"No alcohol? I understand that this Della likes to pick up strange men in bars." Judith asked sneeringly. It was all I could do to keep from jumping up; this woman was seriously starting to annoy me. She had a superior look on her face the whole time Jay talked.

Jay cut her off with a calm statement. "Della rarely drinks. She doesn't like alcohol in any form."

He continued on, "Apparently, Joe was going to come into town this week and tell me that someone had been staying out at the cabin and have us come to check on them. The night that Tate called Elle was when it all blew up. They'd been partying; Joe's son and his date were outside when they heard him yelling and then silence. Next, they heard gunshots; then bullets were flying through the door. Joe went outside, there were more shots, and Buddy went out. He heard Joe yelling, the girl screaming, and after grabbing a rifle, he went outside to check on them. He could hear someone crashing around in the bush, the girl was on the ground, unconscious, and his brother and nephew weren't in sight."

Jay continued, "he ran towards the sounds and got pretty far in before he stumbled over his nephew's body. He could also hear someone moaning up ahead and kept going. He says he was on a bear run, so the going was pretty easy. Buddy found Joe bleeding from a couple of shots to the belly, and as he knelt to check him out, he died. He was going to go get some help when he heard more gunshots, one of which nicked his ear, so he moved sideways, and that's when somebody shot Buddy in the shoulder. He dropped to the ground and played dead. Buddy wasn't sure just how far in he was at that point. Whoever shot him came running up behind him, shone a light at him, and he held his breath until the light went out, then the guy kicked him in the side, hard. He didn't react. As soon as he heard footsteps moving away from him, he got up and started walking further down the trail. "

"Where did they find Buddy? Bill asked.

"He found his way out of the forest to the CC Land road; luckily someone had been out hunting turkey and brought him into town. He had told the hospital that his nephew was dead, shot, somewhere out in the swamp. He said Joe was dead as well but wasn't too sure where he was exactly."

Jay paused in his story long enough to eat more of his lunch and then continued telling us that he'd called Lee as soon as he'd left the hospital. And then I'd called about the tree lying across the road, and if I hadn't told him that Bill and I were coming back to town, he would have told us to come back in.

Lee interrupted him and asked, "Did Buddy mention Della or anything about her?"

Jay replied, "No, he was in a lot of pain when I talked to him and was also pretty weak. He wanted to tell me as much as possible before they took him into surgery. By the time I left, the pain meds were working on him pretty well, and he started sounding a little silly. He kept talking about a ghost, someone who'd gone away long ago and was back again to get his revenge." He paused looked around at us, and continued, "If you guys have finished, I'd like to get someone out to Elle's place and make sure it's OK. Lee, you said you could have some of your people go with Bill to the cabin and check it out." Lee nodded and motioned towards Judith, who'd sat down and was eating quietly and listening to all of this.

"Judith is a sniper with some special training; she's a good backup person. I'd like her to be in charge out there."

Jay nodded and looked at Bill and me, and when he nodded, I did as well. I was scared but didn't want to stay behind. This was my home, Nana's home we were talking about.

"Elle, did you happen to bring your Ruger?" he asked, "make sure you have your quick-loader with you as well and get a flak jacket from one of the guys out there," motioning to the main room. Judith, I assume you've got something similar and will wear it. Bill, we still have that special x-large one you bought us a while back; go ahead and get it. And then let's get going. From what the doctor told me, Buddy should be out of surgery in the next hour or so, and I'd like to talk to him again."

Lee stood up then and said, "I just want to make sure we're all on the same page here. Judith is in charge when you get there. Elle, you don't have any police experience, so I'd like you to stay back, and as soon as Judith clears the house, you can go in. Bill, I want you and Judith to take turns covering each other. You know the drill." Turning to Jay, he added, "Do you have anyone else who can accompany them? I'd feel better if the area could be cleared completely."

Jay shook his head for a second, then turned to Hank and asked if he could go out with us. Hank nodded and then added, "I don't know Judith personally, but I've heard a lot about her", inclining his head toward her, "She's got a good reputation."

By the time the detritus from the lunch had been cleared away and it had been decided on who was riding where and with whom, supplies had been gathered together, another half hour had gone
by.
Skat had taken the opportunity to nap in the corner, and Elle was tempted to join her.

Chapter 17

His safe place had been defiled, and now he had nowhere to go, so he'd come here.

This house was vacant, no one had been there for a couple of days; it waited, silent and patient for its people to come back.

The watcher watched and waited along with the house. It was past time for the people to return to the house, past time for it to wake up. She was coming back, he knew it, the house knew it, but it it didn't want him in there. He'd tried, but the house had known he was there, and when the dog had come out at him, he'd had to retreat, defeated for the moment. Then she'd been there and had taken the dog away, so he tried to get inside again. This time the house had attacked and had thrown him off the back porch, and he was hurt again.

But he was patient and knew that SHE would return. And this time, he was prepared.

I really wasn't pleased to be the passenger on the ride out; I still hadn't warmed up to Judith; her air of supercilious superiority was grating, but it made more sense for me to ride with Judith and let Hank ride out with Bill. I was so hoping the house was still there and not trashed.

The ride to the house was silent; both of us lost in our thoughts. The only comment that Judith had made was to tell me to let her know when they were getting close. I had agreed, and then we'd both lapsed into silence. Judith was following Bill's car when she suddenly braked to a stop and pulled over.

"Do you see that?" she asked, motioning towards the road ahead and to the right. "I caught a glimpse of something that sparkled in the sunlight, catching something reflective in the tree up there."

I looked but couldn't see anything.

"Right there, about 15 feet up in that maple tree." Judith continued, "See. Something is reflecting light at us. Call Hank and tell him something is in the tree; it looks like a mirror reflection."

I grabbed my phone and dialed, but before I could hit send, the car ahead of us suddenly swerved and started to zig-zag back and forth. There were popping sounds, and I felt myself pushed towards the floor.

"Get down, down, on the floor, and call for help. Don't move out of here." Judith ordered as she opened the driver's door and flung herself out. "Tell them shots fired." She stood up, with the car door in front of her, facing the tree, and fired her Glock.

I could see Bill's car accelerate and throw sand up from the rear tires as he sped away before she ducked down under the dash. And I could hear Judith's gun as I dialed Jay's number and told him that shots had been fired at Bill's car. Before I could answer any more questions, Judith was back in the car and had thrown the car into reverse, stepped on the gas, and then twisted the steering wheel, turning us around so fast we were fishtailing down the road away from where we'd been.

It happened so fast that I barely registered what had happened. I was suddenly jerked to the side as the back windshield shattered, and something thumped into the back of my seat, where I'd been sitting seconds before, and then I was jarred forward.

"Shit, shit, shit", was all I heard from Judith as we continued to speed down the road. "Are you hurt?" she asked as she accelerated, driving faster than was really safe on the hard-packed road.

I could feel the car tires grabbing at the road and then skidding a little, not getting the traction needed due to the sandy road surface.

"I'm OK," I answered, shaken by the shattered window and the thump on the back of my seat. I was figuring out that we'd been fired at and the thump I'd felt was a bullet hitting the back of the seat after shattering the back window.

"As soon as we can, we'll stop, but I want to get further down before we pull over. Any place safe for that close by here?"

I only took a few seconds to think and replied, " Turn right, as soon as we get to the main road, there's an old gas station there." My voice shaking as the full import of what had just happened sunk in.

It was only seconds later that Judith pulled into the abandoned gas station. Once upon a time, it had been a busy, bustling gas station with a small souvenir shop. It was advertised as the Last Chance Gas before you hit the forest, but it had been closed for many years. Someone had purchased it at one point with the idea of opening a restaurant but had run out of money before they'd gotten much farther along than pulling the old holding tanks out of the ground. The area where the tanks had been, bare ground just a few short years ago, was now covered with slash pines and various bushes. The pavement had cracks with weeds growing out in many places. It had only taken a short time for the forest to regain and take over the former gas station.

When Judith got out of the car, I went to join her but discovered that I couldn't even stand. I was shaking so badly, and my legs felt like jelly, so I opened the car door and put my head down between my knees to see if that would help. It was then that I saw the bullet sitting on the car seat and the hole where the bullet had punched through the seat back. If I hadn't been jerked to the side, that bullet could have hit me. It was only then I remembered that Skat was still in the back seat I tore open the back door and found Skat lying on the floorboards, covered in glass but unhurt.

It was just too much, and when I tried to stand up again, I found myself sitting instead. So I leaned against the car and seconds later felt Skat sitting beside me, cuddling up to my side, shaking almost as much as me, and craving the closeness.

By the time Jay and the others got to the station, I had finally managed to calm down enough to get up. Nothing in my life had ever prepared me for being shot at on purpose. And it wasn't something I wanted to experience again, ever. I'd been out in the forest when hunters were out and heard the rifles, and those times, I'd just left the forest. Not everyone hunts in season.

And to see the evidence, sitting beside me on the car seat, felt unreal. First, I'd been pushed down seconds before Judith told me to duck, then I'd been jerked to the side just before the bullet came through the back of the car, and I knew Nana had done the shoving. There was no other explanation.

Jay ran over to where I was standing, holding onto the side of the car, and grabbed me in a big hug. He rested his chin on my hair and held on for a second. I melted into his embrace, the last of the adrenaline easing away as he rocked me. It felt so good just to be hugged by my big brother.

"You're OK?" he asked as he let me go.

"I am now, but I think we're going to be getting a call from Mom shortly," I answered, "I got shoved to the floor and then jerked aside by Nana just as the bullet came through the back window'. As I finished my sentence, I heard my phone ring, "Who let the Dogs Out ."I keep that unique ring for my mother. It drives her up the wall sometimes, but she was always asking us, 'Who let the dogs out?' when we were growing up.

"Hi, Mom," I answered, "I'm OK. Did Nana yank my chain?" Mom made wind chimes for each of us and hung them by chains in the yard. When Nana was still alive, she loved to tell tall tales and 'yank our chain', and then she'd laugh. After she passed away, she started yanking the chains and making the chimes sing when one of us was in trouble or had something happen to us. When Jay was shot, his chain rang; when Kay's husband passed away, her chain rang. Just like when I found the body of the first young woman, my chain had rung. I listened momentarily, and "I'm alright, really, and Jay is right here as well." Mom then told me that someone had called asking for me, and he'd hung up on her when she asked who it was. She didn't recognize either the voice or the number he was calling from. "I'm going to hand the phone over to Jay, and you can tell him about that as well, OK? Love you." Before I handed the phone over, I told Jay what Mom had just said about the mystery caller.

"She's fine, a little shaken up, but OK. I'll tell you about it later; right now, we need to see if we can figure out what's going on. Elle never reached the house; someone was waiting by the turnoff and started shooting at the cars. I'll see if I can get more manpower over here, but I need to get going for now. Can you write down the phone number of the guy that called? I'll call you back in a little while to get it. I need to get going here." He listened for another minute and finished the call by telling her he'd drop by later. He handed me back the phone and walked over to where Judith was standing and talking to Lee. It had taken me that long to realize he was there as well. Bill was standing very still by all of them and observing, almost as if he was memorizing all that was going on, and I got a stray thought that this could end up in one of his books. We heard what sounded like a four-wheeler coming through the woods. Everyone's head whipped around, and I noticed that Jay and Lee had their hands on their holsters, but Judith had already pulled her gun out and pointed it towards the woods where the ATV was coming from. I figured she didn't want to be shot at again, without being able to shoot back immediately.

I could make out a trail right there, and sure enough, that's where the ATV was coming from. Driving it was Tate. I had no idea he had an ATV or even used it. Jay was standing beside Judith and put his hand out and pushed her hand, with the gun, pointing it towards the ground.

We headed towards Tate, but before we could get to him, he was off the ATV and walking towards us. As he got closer, I could see the remains of the bruise on his forehead from the other night, but he had fresh contusions on the left side of his face, and dried blood had run down and dripped on his collar.

We could hear him swearing from across the parking lot, and the words he was using were pretty choice. Jay reached him first, The words he was using were not polite either. Jay reached him first and grabbed him as he folded at the knees. And then I noticed that the blood on his collar wasn't the only blood on him. He'd been shot in the shoulder, and as Jay eased him to the ground, he passed out. Judith pushed Jay away and started to pull the collar away from his neck, exposing a narrow, bloody ridge running right across the top of his shoulder. Whoever had shot him had managed to put a nice little crease right above his collarbone.

"Get me something I can put on top of this," she yelled out, "I need a compress." I pulled off my outer shirt, folded it, and handed it to her. Luckily, I'd put a shirt over my tank top before we'd left the house. She took the shirt from me and pressed down on the bloody crease and then we watched as Tate regained consciousness again.

"Some blasted idjit's tramping around the woods firing at anything that moves. You need to get out there and do something, Sheriff," he exclaimed, and then continued, "Ever since word got out about them girls being found out at the cabin, those Edmond boys have been rampaging around my cabin, and the old Mathrey cabin shooting at everything that moves. You know there's always been bad blood between them."

Jay just shook his head, and walked away, muttering under his breath, before he got over to the car, but Bill had beaten him there, and was already on the radio, telling the office that they needed to be on the lookout for the Edmond boys. Although calling them boys was a misnomer as they were in their 30s or 40s. They were well known for causing mischief in town and around, but I'd never heard of them going out with guns and shooting up the forest before. Their usual routine was getting drunk and beating on each other if they couldn't find anyone else to beat on, but both had a long-standing grudge against Buddy and Joe. So it wasn't surprising to hear that they'd been out at the cabin and shooting it up. Someone once said that they had a total of two brain cells between them, and if one was awake, the other couldn't think. Jay walked back towards Tate and faced him as he said, "I want you to go into town to get that shoulder looked at; you lost a fair amount of blood, and with the knock you took the other night, it wouldn't hurt to get checked out." Jay looked at Tate as he said this.

"I'm just fine, no need to go have some doctor looking at me. I got things to do out here, and I can take care of myself just fine." Tate responded, "Sides which the dogs need takin' care of. I can't stay shut up while I get myself doctored up. I can rest jest fine out there. I got my gun and the dogs."

"I would feel a lot better if you let yourself get looked at and have the shoulder bandaged," Jay said. The two men faced each other as they tried to stare each other down, but in the end, Tate wavered, "If'n it'll make you feel better, I'll go into town, but only if Elle goes out and takes care of them dogs." With that, Tate turned and walked away towards the cars.

I wasn't crazy about doing it, but I knew he had a soft spot for his dogs and wouldn't rest easy unless he knew they were OK.

"I'll just go ahead and feed them and shut them in the cabin if you like Tate," I said, "but someone's going to have to drive me out there and back. And I'm not getting on that ATV to do it."

"They'se already inside, but they need a break to go out and pee," he replied, "Their food's on the counter by the stove if they haven't found it and eaten it yet. And bring in their water bucket, they always need a drink after they eat."

After a bit of discussion, it was decided that Jay would go into town with Bill, Lee would take Jay's truck and drive me out to Tate's place, and Judith would follow them back into town. The car had to be taken care of even if it was government issue.

Lee took me out to Tate's place and I gathered the dogs together. It took a little persuasion, but they eventually got into the vehicle thanks mostly to Skat and Blue leading the way.

By the time we got back to town, the dogs were lying on the backseat in a pile of fur. The largest dog, Finn, an Irish wolfhound, was on the bottom, with Blue and Skat on top, and then the smallest dogs, Chico and Sammy, who could have been a dog show, all in one small package, lying on the floorboards. Lee got out of the car and left me with the dogs. Before I got out of the car, I told the dogs I was going inside to arrange a ride, and then we'd head out. By the time I got inside the police station, Lee had already started telling about what they'd found out at Tate's.

As soon as Lee finished telling what they'd found, I asked Jay how Tate was doing; I'd been concerned about him, especially after seeing the dogs loose and the blood on the door jamb.

"He's being stitched up right now. They want to keep him overnight. He lost a lot of blood and coupled with the head injury and his age, they're keeping him in there under some very stringent protests on his part". Jay looked over at Lee, who was bent over a table and showing something on a map to Judith and continued, "What do you want to do with the dogs? "

" I didn't want to leave them out there; it was creepy. Someone had tried to get into the cabin, but the dogs kept them out. Blue probably chased whoever away, and the other dogs guarded the cabin. I could take them to Mom's but would rather go to my place." Jay shook his head, "I'd rather you weren't out there right now. We need to get that tree cleared out, and even with the dogs there, you're my little sister, and I'd just rather you were closer in."

"Thanks, Jay, by the way," with that, I stepped away from Jay and motioned at him to come a little closer, away from everyone in the office, "have you had any weird stuff happening lately? It's not Nana stuff, but I feel like someone is watching me"
Jay nodded, "and?"
" It's disquieting, almost like someone's there and yet not; it's an empty feeling?"

"I have, actually, the other day when Hank and I were at Del's place. It felt like some one was watching us, but I put it down to where we were and what Del was doing. What he does is seriously creepy, I don't mind saying."

"Well, the other day at the house, I felt like someone was watching, but I was taking care of Skat and figured that was why I felt like that. It's creeping me out. I wish we could find out what is going on right now. "Just then, my phone rang with Mom's distinct ring. "Hi, Mom. I'm doing OK now. I have lots of stuff to tell you." I listened for a minute and, looking over at Jay, started laughing silently and pointed to my phone. "Just a sec, Mom, let me run it by Jay, K?" Putting my hand over the phone, "Mom was asking how Tate was and told me to bring all the dogs with me today, so can someone give me a ride?" Jay nodded, and I got back on the phone. "Tate's getting stitched up, and they want to keep him overnight to observe him. He's not thrilled about that one, but he knows I have his dogs. Are you sure, with Skat, and your dogs, that's a lot? OK, I'm arranging a ride, but I'll stop and pick up some dog food. Thanks, Mom," and I hung up the phone. "You know we have a awesome mother, don't you?" to Jay, and then continued, "She also said that she's got dinner arranged and to tell you that Lee, Judith, and Hank are welcome for dinner along with you and Suzanne as well. She just needs a head count in about an hour."

Jay just laughed, "I'll tell them, but I know Suzanne will be glad to have someone else cook. She's swamped right now with prom coming up and is pushing herself. I told her to take it a little easy, but she says she's fine. BTW, Bill wanted to talk to you; he said he has a truck you can borrow until you get a replacement for yours." With that, he stopped and yelled for Bill to come on over to them.

As Bill walked over to them, he reached into his pocket and pulled out a set of keys.

"I figure you need a vehicle while you organize a replacement for your truck, so I had my farm truck brought in, and you're welcome to use it as long as you need it." With that, he handed me a set of keys and pointed out the window to a red truck outside, "It's the red one right there;

it's got 4-wheel drive and lots of space in the crew cab so that the dogs can rest easy in the back seat." I walked over to the window that looked out and saw what looked to be a brand-new red Ford sitting in front of the building.

"Ummm, Bill, is that the one?, as I pointed to it. Bill walked up beside me and looked. "That's the one."

"It doesn't look much like a farm truck to me; in fact, it looks brand new. I can't accept the loan of something that I'll probably scratch up the next time I head out into the bush."

"It's not that new. I bought it last year, and it sits at the house most of the time. You need a truck, I've got one, and you can use it as long as you need to. It's already scratched up and even has a couple of dents if that'll make you feel better." with that, he walked away, and I realized that he didn't want any effusive thanks but was just being generous in his offer. As I was standing there, Jay walked up to me and looked out at the truck. He inclined his head down and whispered, "Just say thanks and figure that your truck getting torched will end up in one of his books, and this is his way of 'paying' you for the story. Don't worry, I think he can afford you to use it for a while." I turned around and said "Thank you" to Bill as I headed out the door to check out the truck. It only took a few moments for me to get the dogs transferred from the car to the truck after I put down the back seats to make a flat platform. Just as I was getting ready to drive away, Bill came out and told me that the truck had another feature, a remote start, and showed me. He added, "Just in case you take Skat with you, it'll run for about 10 minutes, and you can restart it once, but that's it. And it's nice to get the truck cooled off before you get in." He turned and walked back into the police station. I got into the truck, belted myself in, and headed to my folk's place. By the time I got there, the dogs were ready to get out and stretch and pee. I let them all out, and Skat took over as hostess, or at least that's what it looked like. She barked at the dogs, and they followed her to the back of the house. I just shook my head and followed them back. By the time I got to the back, Mom had already opened the gate to the backyard, and the dogs had followed Skat in, found the water dish, and were busy getting a welcome drink.

It didn't take long before Jay and the rest came, by which time I'd helped Mom get the dinner finished. When Suzanne texted that she was on the way, we got the Cottage Pie, or as this family called it, Rustic Pot Roast, into the oven to finish cooking. Mom had made two large ones, and it didn't take us long to demolish both pans. The dogs had made themselves at home, finding various pieces of rugs to lay down on, and Jay got the family caught up in what had been happening.

It did get a little crowded on my bedroom floor that night. I was used to having one dog to trip over, and that night, I had five stretched out on the floor. And found out that five dogs woofing, snoring, and whimpering in their sleep means that the human does not sleep all that soundly. At least I didn't, but the dogs did.

The following day, just after I had gotten the dogs fed and taken care of, Jay called to tell us that Tate was being released and wanted to return to his cabin. I offered to go and pick him up and take the dogs with us. After dropping off Tate and the dogs and ensuring everything was OK at the cabin, I returned to the house and met Jay. "Hey Elle," Jay called out, "feel like a drive out to see Miss Mavis? I want to make sure she's OK if the Edmond boys are out being idiots." I just looked at him and walked over to the truck, and Skat followed me as I climbed in. She wasn't about to let me get far away at the moment.

I was also happy to go with him to see Miss Mavis. She was a well-known character and could be counted on to tell the truth as she saw it.

Chapter 18

Miss Mavis was a distant relation to the Mathreys and had been as much a grandmother to Joe and Buddy as Vivian had been. And she would champion them every time she could. She lived on the outskirts of town, and visiting her was always an experience.

It was always easy to see when someone had gotten new furniture in town. The old furniture was handed off to a grown child, cousin, or other family member deemed less fortunate. The replaced furniture often wound into a downward spiral, with any semi-decent recliners ending up on Miss Mavis Jar's porch.

She would sit, smoke her pipe, drink her 'shine' out of a quart jar, and wax philosophical, imparting her wisdom to all. She was a big champion of 'her boys' as she called Vivian's grandsons, Buddy and Joe.

On this particular day, she was sitting, in state, on the newest recliner to grace her porch. Elle counted 4 of them, arranged side by side, with cats sitting and laying in piles on the three to the right of Miss Mavis. They were all faded from sun and weather and ranged in colors from a mauve on the end to a sage green on the newest one. A fifth recliner had been pushed off the edge of the porch, where it would remain until one or another of her many relatives hauled it off to the recliner graveyard. I'd often wondered how many recliners had met their final rewards there. But I'd never been brave enough to either ask or to explore her backyard in case that's where they ended up.

As she and Jay drove up, Miss Mavis waved at them to come on in. The gate and fence had been recently repaired, and fresh wire and posts held up the gate that usually sagged in or out depending on the last person through.

As Elle pushed open the gate, a big blue tick hound came baying out at her. She jumped for a second until she recognized Jasper; he'd been one of the 'found' dogs and had ended up staying with Miss Mavis. He stopped short just before he got to her and then flopped onto his back, wiggling in the sand with a big ol' grin on his face.

"He's worthless as a guard dog but comes in handy, scaring the bears and cats away, "she called out. "Come on up and tell me the latest bad news. I got some funerals to plan and a boy to nurse and don't have time to waste on no foolishness."

Elle and Jay made their way past Jasper, who jumped up and tried to block them from going up the walkway. He wanted them to stop and rub his belly or his ears; he wasn't too particular about which one.

Elle stopped and gave Jasper the petting he was demanding as Jay walked up to the porch; he took off his hat as a measure of respect to Miss Mavis.

"I'm sorry to bother you, Miss Mavis, but I need to know if you've seen anything strange out behind you in the woods. Anything at all."

"Jasper's been bayin' a lot lately, but I just figured it was that time of year; he don't like the bears taking a shortcut through what he thinks is his. A few nights back, I heard something thrashing out around the back, and Jasper sounded off about that, but he didn't want to go outside at all. Dog's a nuisance with his barking sometimes, but he usually takes off and chases whatever is out there.

He'd been limping around for a day, so I figured that was why he didn't want to go chasin' after whatever it was. Think it had anything to do with the shoot-up at the boy's house? "

"Thanks, Miss Mavis, that helps. I don't know if it has anything to do with what happened at the cabin. Tate says he's seen lights out and some shooting going on out there. Have you heard anything like that?"

"Nope, but then again, my ears don't work as good as they used to. "

As Elle finally made her way past Jasper, she noted that not only did Miss Mavis have her little table with her 'shine' jar sitting beside her, but also within easy reach was a shotgun, a Mossberg 12 gauge. One that had been recently cleaned and looked ready to use. Jay had noticed it as well. Usually Miss Mavis kept a .22 rifle handy, at least the other times Elle had been out here.

She claimed to be a crack shot with a .22 and used it to shoot squirrels when she was in the mood for a good stew.

"Notice you got the Mossberg out, Miss Mavis. Not using the .22 these days? "

"After Jasper took on so the other night and didn't go outside, I decided to get the shotgun out and keep it handy. This'un will knock a bear on his butt and make him think twice."

With that, Jay inclined his head and told her thanks. And we left, Jasper, escorting us to the gate. where he waited while we went through. After getting into Jay's vehicle, he turned to Elle.

"There's more going on there than Miss Mavis is letting on. Did you notice the dog wasn't limping?"

"I got that too," Elle said, "He was pretty frisky, and Miss Mavis looked a tad nervous. The only other time I remember seeing her with a shotgun was when she tree'd the Edmond boys after they trespassed behind her cabin a few years back. That was before you moved back here, and old Sheriff Piggott had a heck of a time persuading them to climb down; they swore she would get them if they did. They'd been coon hunting and got themselves turned around somehow, they said. It had nothing to do with all the beer they'd been drinking that day. Did you see, she also had a revolver tucked under the cushion on that next recliner. I noticed her hand move a cushion a little as we were coming in the gate. I just hope it wasn't the .44; the last time she shot that one, the gun jumped out of her hand and broke the window behind her."

"How do you know that?" Jay asked.

"I was at the hardware store when one of her grandsons stopped in for some window glass, and he was telling everyone about it. He thought it was funny cause she'd been shooting at the Edmond boys and missed them. A couple of weeks later, she 'treed' the Edmond boys when they got 'lost' hunting. You don't fool with Miss Mavis."

Jay just nodded and got that look on his face that Elle recognized as him starting to put pieces together in his mind.

They drove on back into town and he dropped her off at the truck Bill had lent her with the admonition to should keep her phone and her Ruger handy at all times.

Elle wasn't about to argue with him.

Chapter 19

Jay finally cleared it so I could go back to my house. Bill and some other guys had gotten the tree off the driveway and checked out the house and surrounding area. There were no more signs of anyone trying to break in. With the warning from Jay to keep my phone charged and on me and to call if there was anything off, I was finally able to go home. I had to admit it was a relief to be in my own space again, and Skat seemed to be content as well. She'd patrolled the outside, peed in a few places, and then came back up on the wide porch to sit. I'd stopped at the store on my way home to stock up on a few necessities. I'd also visited Della in the hospital a couple of times; physically, she was getting better, but she'd been so traumatized from that night at the cabin that she was still not communicating very well. I knew she recognized me, but it was hard to determine what she was saying. Something that had happened to her had left her trapped in her mind. She seemed capable of saying only one phrase, 'bad dels back,' and she would repeat it whenever you asked her how she was doing. The doctors all seemed to be in agreement that she'd be fine but needed to get over the trauma of that night. No one knew how she'd ended up at the cabin either. Buddy was recovering from his gunshot wound but wasn't going to be released soon. Joe and his son's funerals were scheduled, but Miss Mavis wanted to wait until Buddy had been released from the hospital before that happened.

I smelled the unmistakable odor of soured meat when I opened the fridge. Before all the events that took me out of my house for a few days, I'd pulled some hamburger meat from the freezer and put it into the fridge to thaw, but it had gone off, way off and stunk up the fridge, as the package had also leaked some blood. After smelling the milk as well, I realized it was also sour. Cleaning the refrigerator out was my top priority. I hated to throw the milk out, but did. I knew Eric would be looking for something sweet when he came home from college, so I threw a couple of coffee cakes together. I'd learned long ago that cakes didn't last long when Eric and his friends were around. And by making them, I was ahead of the game by at least one dessert. They'd also freeze well. After baking and cooling the cakes, I did a quick clean and relaxed on the back porch with a cup of tea. I'd already begged off work at Fred's for a few days, but I knew I had to go in soon.

While sitting there, Skat sat beside me on her cushion. She seemed content. She was also relishing the quiet and needed to rest up. Not only had she played a lot with Mom and Dad's dogs, but she'd also played hostess to Tate's dogs the night they spent with us.

I'd missed sitting out here; this porch had many great memories. The times I sat out here with Nana, enjoying a cup of herbal tea while I was pregnant, or sitting in the rocking chair nursing Eric when he'd wake me up in the middle of the night. He'd latch on and nurse so quietly as if he was absorbing the peace and tranquility of the area. Later on, when he was teething or fussy, just sitting out here seemed to calm him down. I'd sit and talk for hours on end out here with Nana, her imparting a little wisdom to me but mostly listening to my girlish dreams. I'd come out here when I received the last letter back from Lee and cried my eyes out sitting in the lounge.

I don't know how long we'd been sitting and enjoying the quiet before Skat sat straight up and gave a very low-pitched growl. She looked out towards the side of the house and seemed to be staring at something. Just then, I heard a car coming down the driveway, and I grabbed my phone and went to look. Skat immediately rose and walked beside me as I went to the back stairs. I knew I'd locked the front door, but I decided to peek around the corner to see who was coming down the drive. After the events of the past few days, I was feeling extra cautious.

I can't say I was completely surprised to see it was Lee. We hadn't had a chance to speak except briefly with all the other events that happened. And that was all the FSIU stuff. As soon as Skat saw who it was, she moved out in front of me and kept herself just a few feet in front. I watched her in some bemusement; this was a new behavior for her and one I rather liked. She'd gone from hiding behind me to walking beside me and now was placing herself out in front and between me and what she perceived as a possible threat.

"Lee," I greeted him, "is there something new?"

He shook his head, " I just wanted to come out and check to make sure everything was all right here. I know you spent some time with your folks, and Jay cleared the house. I wanted to talk with you about something else.""Come on up, and I'll make us some tea. I just baked some coffee cakes, and they should be cool enough to eat.

With that, I turned and walked back to the steps, Skat staying right behind me, placing herself between Lee and me. I had to admit I was getting a kick out of her new behavior. Lee followed but then stopped and looked out towards the woods at the same time that Skat stopped and did her low-pitched growl as she looked in the same direction. She then walked over to Lee and stood beside him, on point, the low, almost inaudible growl continuing. I followed over to them and looked out past the cleared backyard towards the palmetto's and trees in the woods. I was used to seeing the occasional bear or raccoon, but I couldn't see anything. And then I realized there was no noise, birds, rustling, nothing. It was eerie. And disquieting.

I looked over at Lee as he looked at me with a questioning look. I noticed his right hand drifting down to the gun he had holstered on his hip, a gun I hadn't even noticed until now. He turned towards me, put his left hand to his lips to be quiet, and motioned towards the woods. He then motioned me to go inside, waving his left hand at me as a shot rang out. I cut and ran towards the open doorway as Skat ran past me into the house. As I looked back at Lee, he'd dropped down and was scooting backward to get behind the chairs I had there. As soon as I got inside, I got away from the open doorway and windows and entered the hallway. By the time I made it in the house, Lee had also come inside. I had my phone in my hand and dialed Jay before Lee got up and stood beside me.

"Jay, I was just outside on the back porch, and someone shot a gun. Lee's here, and we got inside; there was only one shot." I stopped and listened for a moment to Jay and then handed Lee the phone.

"Did you see anything?" he asked just before he took the phone from me. I shook my head no and said, "The first thing I noticed was Skat growling and looking toward the back woods." With that, Lee took the phone and talked to Jay. I heard him say something about staying put until Jay and Judith could get out there. As he talked to Jay, I got down on the floor with Skat and petted her. Her behavior had alerted us, and whoever or whatever was out there had only shot once.

"We need to stay away from any windows or doors," Lee said, after hanging up from Jay, "Jay's coming out with Judith to check it out. Do you have any rooms without windows?" I shook my head no, "this hallway is about it; Nana liked having large windows in every room."

"Then we're staying put until Jay and reinforcements get here. He said it wouldn't take long." I just nodded and sat down with Skat, cuddling up as close as she could without getting in my lap. I could see into the living room from my spot, and that's when I noticed where the bullet had hit. A nice big hole, just barely beside a framed embroidery piece Nana's mother had made. I turned towards Lee and pointed at the hole. "My great great grandmother embroidered that picture, and whoever shot at us just barely missed it. From the size of the hole, it wasn't a .22 either, probably something like a .357 ."

Lee looked at me, "How can you tell?"

"I've got a Ruger and shoot .38 caliber bullets. I know what size hole they make in a piece of plywood and how big a hole a .22 makes. Jay ensured I knew how to handle guns before getting my conceal carry permit".

As we stood looking at the hole, the frame of the picture slipped over and covered most of the bullet hole in the wall. I then knew Nana was around somehow, she'd managed to save the picture by sliding over the frame just enough that the bullet missed it.

It seemed to take forever, but it was just minutes before I heard sirens, and I knew Jay was on his way. The hallway had started to feel claustrophobic, with Lee, Skat, and I huddled together away from both ends, as far away as possible from any possible openings. All we'd heard was the one shot, but if someone was outside watching, they could easily shoot again.

Just as I heard the sirens getting louder, which meant that Jay had turned into the driveway, I heard footsteps clomping up the stairs onto the back porch, and a voice called out "Miss Elle, you in there? Sorry, Grady tripped on a log, and his gun went off; I think it hit your house."

I recognized the voice; it was Earl Edmond, one of the two almost infamous Edmond boys, instigator of more lame pranks and idiocies than many people in our town. They were known for their drunken brawls outside Fred's after imbibing three too many beers, luckily they usually only beat on each other. They were also known for being terrified of their mother. As soon as I heard Earl's voice, I came out. I knew it was Earl, as he had a pronounced lisp, which led some people to think he wasn't too bright. Those people would have been mistaken, as Earl was maybe not book-smart, but instead could navigate anywhere in the forest without getting lost, so long as he didn't let Grady lead him astray and so long as they weren't 'lost.'

    Lee made a frantic grab for me, but I knew the only danger I was in now was from excessive apologizing. By the time I got out into the living room, Earl stood with his nose up against the sliding glass door, trying to see in; not a pretty sight, but a semi-welcome one.

    As I got closer, I saw that Grady was coming across the lawn and I stepped out onto the porch with Earl, just as Jay rounded the corner with his gun drawn.

    "Goddamnit, What in the tarnation are you doing?" He yelled as he holstered his gun and walked towards Earl. Lee just looked back and forth from Jay to me in confusion, as he'd also drawn his gun. I motioned towards him to put his gun away.

    "It's OK. I'll explain later, but we're in no danger unless Grady trips again." We'd all had dealings with the 'boys' as they were known around here. Basically harmless, they were a bit of a joke. Hard-working, reliable, sweet, and gentle for the most part, but if they got drunk, they got stupid. Earl was the younger of the two and got led into more transgressions by Grady without questioning him.

    Both boys, as I said, were terrified of their mother, even though they were adults. Grady had been a couple of grades ahead of me in school, while Earl followed behind by a couple. Their momma, Dovie Edmond was a fierce mama bear when it came to the boys and would shelter them as much as possible while simultaneously meting out punishment. I had seen her smack Earl across the back with a wooden spoon, which broke on impact, when he didn't step aside and make way for a pregnant woman as quickly as Dovie thought he should.

I watched Grady emerge from the tree line and run across the backyard. He tripped again and fell flat on his face, but at least this time, he wasn't carrying his gun. Grady came up screaming and started on a dead run towards the house. By the time he reached the steps to the porch, Lee and Jay had both gotten to the bottom and stopped him before he came up. Earl had also gotten down to the ground by the simple expedient of jumping from the top step to the bottom of the steps.

"He's out there; I saw him; he's gonna kill us all," Grady babbled as he fell towards Earl, "he told me we're all dead, all dead."

"Whoa, wait a minute, saw who? " Jay asked, looking at Grady and then enunciating slowly and clearly, "Who did you see?"

Grady just looked at him with a totally confused look in his eyes and shook his head. "the bad man, the one you're looking for, the bad one who took Della." He turned a little, looked up at Earl, and very quietly said, "We need to go get Momma; she needs to get safe." He stood up then, with an odd sort of dignity, and looked at Jay, "Can you see that Momma's OK? She needs to get safe." Even with the tear tracks down his face, he still stood tall. And then my heart broke when he looked up at Earl and said very quietly, "I need to go get fresh pants on; I messed my pants when he scared me." I then looked closer at Grady, and the look on his face and the spreading dark stain on his pants told me and us that whatever had happened in the woods had totally and completely terrified him.

Jay looked over at me, then moved over to my side before leaning down and whispering in my ear, "do you have anything I can put on the cruiser seat so Grady can sit down? I want to give them a ride to their momma's place and ensure she's alright."

I patted him on the arm and turned to go back up the steps to the porch. I had some large leaf bags inside that Jay could spread over the seat to keep them from getting soiled. But as I got to the top, I stopped; there was a prickly feeling on my neck as if someone was staring at me. But when I looked down at the guys, they were huddled together, talking to Earl and Grady. So I shook off the feeling and went to get the plastic bags for Jay.

It didn't take long for Jay and Lee to go and walk around the backyard and look into the tree line, but they found nothing more than the trail the Edmond's had made coming through the bush. The only other thing they spotted was a bear run, but I'd known about that for a long time. Bears tend to make a trail, which they follow through the forest and use often enough that the vegetation stays cleared out.

While they were out looking around, I tried chatting a little with Earl, but Grady was still trapped in his fear. Grady didn't want to talk; he just kept looking down at the ground with occasional glances at the tree line. I got close to Earl and told him I'd gotten a couple of bags to put down on the seat in the police cruiser so that Grady could sit comfortably on the ride out to their momma's. I'd forgotten that Judith had ridden out with Jay, and she was still standing at the corner of the house, keeping an eye out. She'd put her gun back in the holster at the same time Jay and Lee had but had kept herself apart from the rest of us. It had only been a few minutes since Grady came running out of the woods, but it seemed much longer.

By the time Jay and Lee had walked back up the yard to where we were standing at the foot of the stairs, Judith had also come over. She leaned over to me and quietly asked if there was something she could do. She was looking at Grady as she said it, but I told her that it was all good and told her I had leaf bags to spread on the back seat of the cruiser for Grady. I went inside to grab the bags and handed them to her, and she went around the corner to the cruiser. It took a few more minutes, and then Jay, Judith, and the Edmonds left.

Lee and I walked back up the step to the porch, and I collapsed onto one of the chairs. Skat had made herself scarce during all the commotion and had stayed up on the porch, out of the way.

Chapter 20

After sitting on the porch for a few minutes, I went inside to make some tea and bring out one of the coffee cakes I'd made earlier, anticipating that Eric would be coming home as soon as possible. I knew from experience that it would take little time before the cakes and most of the food in the house would go. I made a mental note to go and restock my pantry in the morning. Knowing Eric, he'd already alerted his friends he was coming, which meant they'd all converge on the house and would manage to eat everything remotely edible they could find. I used to call them the ravening horde when they were teenagers cause they could clean out the fridge and pantry faster than a hungry army.

I brought out the tea, cake, and rest of the bottle of Jameson's Mom had brought me, the other week. After all the excitement, I needed something more potent than just a cup of hot Irish breakfast tea. I picked up the bottle, poured a generous dollop into my cup, and held it up to Lee. He shook his head and I picked up my cup and sipped. I guess being an FSIU agent, you got used to being shot at, but it was a new experience for me having a bullet shot into my home, and not one I wanted to repeat. It was bad enough in the woods during hunting season, which is why I never went in when they had idjits hunting and shooting anything that moved. I'd had a couple of bullet holes in my old truck which had luckily missed me.

"So," started Lee, "what can you tell me about the Edmond's? I noticed you and Lee weren't especially upset with Grady or Earl. What's the story with Grady? Is he slow?"

"Short answer: Grady isn't slow; he was traumatized as a kid when he pulled his dying father out of a burning house. Every so often, something sets his PTSD off, and he reverts to being a scared kid again. Someone had set their house on fire and had knocked his father, E.G., out before setting the fire. It was considered suspicious because E.G.'s office was the only room with any measurable fire damage. He'd also been badly beaten before the fire, according to the medical examiner. The sheriff at the time ruled it an accidental death.

"Where were Earl and his mother?"

"At the time of the fire, she was visiting family out of town and had Earl with her. Grady had refused to go with them and stayed back with his Dad. I believe he was around 12 at the time, and he worshipped his father."

I then filled Lee in on more of the story. E.G. Edmond was a former reporter who'd been a big part of the civil rights movement, and one day he'd met Dovie during a protest he was covering. She was barely out of her teens then, and he was more than twice her age. They fell in love and moved here in the late 70's or early 80's. They had Grady and then, a few years later, Earl. E.G. had retired as a reporter but did a lot of freelance writing, and it was well known that he was working on a book in which he was naming names and describing some of the atrocities he'd seen. In the weeks leading up to his death, rumors were flying around town about how descriptive his book would be, and fears about him naming names. At that time, there was a strong Klan presence here, and they didn't like anyone messing around and asking questions.

"Alright, next question.", Lee said, "everyone refers to those guys killed at the cabin as Mathrey, but their last name is Falchion. I asked Jay, but he just said that their mom had taken back her maiden name after her husband had died."

"She did. I don't think it was an especially great marriage. Sheriff Falchion died after he bled to death after somehow stabbing himself with a knife he carried on his hip in a kind of holster. He was well known for using it as intimidation when questioning people. You'd have to ask Jay about any particulars on it. I think I remember someone saying that it was a touch suspicious, his death, that is."

Lee shifted in his chair and stared straight out at the woods. He seemed to be in deep thought, so the next question out of his mouth startled me.

"So", started Lee, "when were you going to tell me about Eric?"

I looked at him, and my mouth gaped open. My head was still back on Grady and how he was doing, so this next question came out of left field and then some.

"What do you mean?"

"Were you pregnant that summer?"

"How do you mean pregnant?"

"I mean, were you pregnant when we were together?" Lee said in an accusing tone of voice.

I just looked at him, dumbfounded.

"I didn't find out I was pregnant until after you left."

Lee just looked at me with a look comprised equally of distrust and disbelief. I was stupefied, my mind unable to skip over what had just happened outside, and then to get into this conversation, I wasn't prepared, and had thought we'd be talking about the Edmond brothers, not my son.

"I saw the pictures of Jay and Eric in his office and asked him who the young boy was in the photos. He just told me it was his nephew, Eric, and made it plain the subject was off limits."

"He did? What did he say? I'm sorry, I'm confused."
"Jay said that his name was Eric and that if I wanted to

know anything more, I had to ask his mother. I asked who his mother was, and he said he'd pass on the question to Eric's mother."

"I see," I said,

"While we were in the house, I saw all the pictures of Eric on the wall in the kitchen, so I figured you were Eric's mother. So who's the father? "

I just shook my head and replied, " You are. I sent you some letters after I found out I was pregnant, several of them as a matter of fact, but they came back marked return to sender, and my final letter was returned torn into pieces."

"I don't believe you, I never got any letters."

"Well, someone tore up the last letter and sent me the pieces in an envelope with Leave Me Alone printed on the back. I saved it, along with all the other letters that were sent back, with return to sender printed on the envelopes. I kept them for Eric in case he ever wanted to know about his father. At least, I kept them so that he could see I'd tried to tell his biological father that he existed." I got up then and walked into the house. I had the box with the letters tucked away in my closet. I'd not looked at them in years; the hurt and anger from his betrayal had faded long ago. I just placed the letters I'd written over the years to Lee on top of the rest. I had a healthy son who had grown into a man I was proud of.

By the time I returned with the box, Lee was standing at the edge of the porch, looking out over the backyard towards the woods.

"I never got any letters. Are you sure you sent them?" By this time, his voice and attitude had gone beyond disbelief and bordered on nasty.

"Would a postmark on the envelopes convince you?" I asked, "I have all the letters here; you're welcome to look. I also tried calling you, but your mother told me you didn't want anything to do with me. I have no way of proving that I made those calls."

Lee turned around and then looked at me, standing with the plastic shoe box in my hands, with a stack of letters visible through the clear sides.

"I have them all in here; if you want to look at them, come inside." With that, I turned around again, walked into the kitchen, and placed them on the table. I wasn't about to open the box before he came in; I wanted him to see me open it. Not only were the letters he had sent back in there, but also every single letter I'd written him over the years. Nana had encouraged me to write Lee letters, even though he would probably never see them; she'd also counseled keeping them for Eric when he grew up. I'd shared so much of Eric's life in them, from the first time I breastfed him and how it felt and how I'd inhale that wonderful baby smell. I tried to write down each of the firsts as they happened, the good and the bad. From the first time, he slept the entire night through to his first tooth and successful use of the potty chair, his first crush, heartbreak when he didn't get chosen for the baseball team, and his first home run. I wrote letters to Lee when I was so exhausted from lack of sleep, after sitting up with a fretful, achy baby all night, and pretty much any time I had something I wanted to share. Just as I put the box on the table, I heard Lee's cell phone ring. It was a generic ring, one of those rings that come with your phone. I couldn't make out what he was saying, but as he entered the house, I heard him tell the person on the other end that he'd be there.

"That was Jay; he just called to say that they found another body, rather the remains of a woman. Some kayakers found her out on the walking trail by the Burnt Bridge. Jay said you'd know exactly where it was. Could you run me out there, or should I follow you?"

"You can follow me; that way, your car is handy. Let me just put this away and get my shoes." As I motioned towards the box, I felt strongly that I did not want it sitting out. After returning it to my bedroom and placing it in the closet, I grabbed my shoes and a pair of rubber boots. I had no intention of just dropping Lee off and leaving. I wanted to see what or rather who it was out there.

Whatever was happening around here lately was downright scary.

Coming out of the bedroom, I caught Lee looking at my brag wall in the kitchen. Eric had been embarrassed, intrigued, and proud of that wall at various times. I'd tried to capture as many of the big and small moments, the triumphs and trials of Eric's life. When he was a teen, and I could have cheerfully strangled him, it helped me to be able to look at how cute he was as a toddler. I was able to keep the murderous impulses at bay then. Some of the pictures were incredibly precious, and I'd made copies of them and even had them blown up. I especially loved the one of Eric as a 3 or 4 year-old holding up a handful of squashed blackberries for Nana to taste. The contrast of innocence and age was so vivid. Nana had just tasted the berries, lovingly held up to her by Eric, with juice dripping down his hand and arm onto the floor. Her beautiful aged face and wrinkles contrasted so well with that chubby little fist, dripping with juice between his fingers. I was so happy I had the camera in my hand and turned on when I caught that vignette on film. I don't even remember what I was preparing to photograph then. Whatever it was, it wasn't important.

" Are you ready?" I asked, "It'll take a little while to get there. I want to bring in the stuff from the porch. You can follow me out to the bridge."

I'd almost forgotten the tea and cake out on the

porch. If left out, it would attract bugs and maybe some wildlife. I brought the tray into the house and looked at my barely sipped cup of tea with the shot of Jameson in it. I put it into the fridge for later, thinking I might need it. If you can drink plain iced tea, why not drink it with a shot of something good? Waste not, want not.

Chapter 21

I was relieved that Lee was following me out there; I didn't want to be stuck inside a vehicle with him after he questioned me about Eric. His attitude had been borderline antagonistic. As it was, I knew that the conversation wouldn't be easy, but at least the box had been opened up a crack.

As I'd told Lee, it would take a little while to get out to the Burnt Bridge, so named because someone had set a fire under it many years ago, and the soot from the fire had blackened the timbers and supports for the bridge without hurting the structure itself. You don't try to burn green wood. It makes for some angry-looking smoke and the creosote from the green wood burning deposits black tar on any nearby structure.

After I finished putting everything away, I called Skat to me, there was no way I was leaving her behind. She looked a little confused when we came out. I think she was still looking for the old truck, but it didn't take her more than a few seconds to realize which vehicle we were going in. I opened the truck's back door and motioned her to jump in. She hesitated for a second; this truck that Bill had lent us was a little higher than my old truck. But the hesitation was momentary as she gauged the height and jumped into the back seat. I hadn't gotten a new cushion to put down for her, and she let me know with a grumble. She was also used to being in the front seat with me and not in the back with all that room.

I started the truck, and it caught right away, unlike my old one, which sometimes had to be coaxed into starting. I liked this truck, with all the mod cons, including a really efficient air conditioner. I had parked the truck when I had gotten home so that I didn't have to turn around if I wanted to leave in a hurry. As we left I pulled it forward enough that Lee could pull his car up enough that he could turn around to follow me out. On the drive out to Burnt Bridge, I started running some numbers in my head; I wanted to see what I could afford to buy, and I wondered if Bill would let me just buy this truck and make payments. I was so lost in thought that I almost forgot to signal to turn off onto RT. 65. The road into Burnt Bridge was rutty, sandy, and best navigated slowly with a 4WD vehicle. It was slow going from this point, but if Lee was careful, his car should make it, and if not, I could always pull him out. I'd noticed a heavy-duty chain in the back of the truck in the tool case. I was falling more and more for this truck. Skat had noticed when we turned off, and she had felt the turn. She was sitting up, and her nose twitched as she tried to catch a scent. She always knew when we were on our way down to Tate's, either the rhythm of the road or a scent she caught would let her know, and I'd hear a low pitched whine coming from her.

 It had been a few months since I'd been down this particular road, and as always, I was alert not only for road kill but also to see if any of the old roads leading off had been used recently. There were roads cut into the bush, all over the place, some from hunters cutting through, but there were also some old roads or trails leading off that sometimes led to old abandoned homesteads. The county graders had been through here recently, and the road was in good condition; later in the summer, it would become a sand trap if it was dry or quicksand-like when we had rain. Either way, it could become a hazardous drive.

 I also kept a close eye on my rearview mirror, but Lee seemed to be navigating the road just fine. As we approached the bridge, I noticed that someone had been hacking away at the growth on either side of the road and wondered at that.

 Jay, of course, was there, as well as Doc Freitag,

both looking down at a tarpaulin-covered mound. I pulled over beside the ambulance and parked, with Lee parking right behind me. I was going to leave the windows cracked for Skat, but I could tell that the truck would be filled with bugs in short order, so I used the nifty little fob and did a remote start on the truck. This way, not only could I keep the bugs out, but Skat could stay inside in the cool.

When I got to them, Lee had exited his car and passed me. I was there more for curiosity's sake anyway, and it was easier to have Lee follow me out than to try and explain exactly how to get here.

As Jay walked up to me, he took off his hat and wiped his brow on his shirt. It was hot out here, humid and buggy as well. Being this close to the river meant that we were assailed not only by yellow flies but mosquitoes and no-see-ums as well. I knew I'd be sporting quite a few new bites when I left.

Spraying with bug spray didn't help, nor did many of the other 'remedies' people espoused. I knew that because I'd tried the majority of them.

"Hey Lee", he started, "I'm glad you brought Elle out, although I don't think it's anything for the FSIU to get involved with." he continued with that note in his voice, the one that says, I've got bad news, "Some kayaker's stopped to take pictures of the bridge, and spotted something on shore, and went to investigate. They found a woman's body and called it in."

Jay stopped, looked down at the ground, then looked up at me sadly, "it was Mary they found, it looks like she's been dead a couple of days, and her body's already been," he paused, swallowed hard, as if trying to find the right words, "disturbed, by some animals." I was shocked. I hadn't seen Mary for a couple of weeks; she was a fixture in town, almost endlessly walking around from store to store. However, there were also times when she'd hole up in her little trailer, and we wouldn't see her for a while. She'd explain it to you if you asked as the bad times were back, but for the most part, she was pretty nonverbal. Mary was on the austistic spectrum and, for most of her life, had resided at home with her father. Her mother had left when she was just a toddler, and her father had raised her. He'd left her a small annuity when he died, and one of our local attorneys was the guardian ad litem for her. But she was also looked after by our community.

The years hadn't been kind to her, although she retained a look of innocence. I hadn't paid much attention to her as a teen, but even back then, she'd walked everywhere and sometimes made her way out to our special swimming spot. I don't think any of us ever interacted with her. Teens aren't known for being especially kind, Lisele being the exception. Mary would often show up when Lisele was with us and sit there and watch us. I know that Lisele took Mary under her wing and would help her with clothing and baths. Still, after Lisele was murdered, no one helped her until the Methodist church ladies made sure that she had appropriate clothing for the time of year and that it got changed out every few weeks or months. She could and did wear the same outfit for weeks on end, and no one made the mistake of standing down wind of her more than once. The ladies in the church made sure she bathed before getting her fresh clothing, even if she wore it to rags. Many times it was an outfit that my sister-in-law Suzanne had donated. Mary would wander into her store from time to time and would fixate on an item of clothing. She was fiercely independent and insisted on paying her way, usually flashing a wad of cash from her annuity check, once a month. The manager of the Dollar General was in the habit of using her when he'd hire new cashiers. She knew to a penny how much something would cost, with or without tax, and never hesitated to call out the cashier on it.

He used her to weed out the dishonest cashiers.

I was on a nodding, very casual basis of acquaintance with her; I'd say hello or nod as I passed her in the street. She walked everywhere almost incessantly, usually barefoot as well. She also carried a pair of slippers, which she'd put on before going into the stores in town; she took the 'no shoes, no service' sign seriously. I was curious how she'd ended up out here, though, as Burnt Bridge was easily 7 miles out of town. I'd never known her to venture out of town more than a mile or two.

"Doc's going to take her in and see if she find a COD, but it looks like natural causes for right now." For some reason, her death hit me hard; Mary had been a fixture here for a long time, years, in fact. I told Jay I would head back home then, but remembered to ask how Grady was doing.

"He's fine, I dropped him off at his momma's place along with Earl. I also lectured them about tramping through the woods with a gun when it wasn't hunting season. And I confiscated his rifle; I want the FSIU to see if they can compare the rifling on it to the bullets at the Mathrey's cabin, but I don't think it was them. Grady kept mumbling something that sounded a lot like what Della was saying in the hospital when we brought her in."

He paused and took a step back as a particularly strong breeze assailed our noses with the odor of putrefaction from Mary's body, which was in the process of being loaded into the ambulance. With the heat, it didn't take long for any body to start to rot. I didn't envy Doc's drive back into town with that in the back, even with the body zipped into a body bag.

Although we'd only been there a short time, I swore that the stench of rotting flesh was burned into my nostrils. I was tempted to go and find some cheap cologne I could inhale or, better yet, snort.

I shook myself momentarily as I focused on Jay's last comment. "What do you mean, it sounded like what Della had said? Grady also said something about the bad man being back, the same one that hurt Della. Is that what you mean?"

Just then, we were interrupted by Doc Freitag, saying peremptorily,

"Jay, I don't think Mary died of natural causes; after we got her in the body bag, I grabbed her purse to take with us. It was really heavy so I looked inside. She had a half bottle of orange soda and a half bottle of grape soda. I know she didn't like Grape, but if someone bought her a bottle, she'd drink it really fast and then drink or eat something after so she could get the taste of the Grape out of her mouth. And since both were only half gone, I put both bottles in evidence bags." Turning to Lee, she added, "I'd like the FSIU to take both bottles and check the contents and get any prints off the outsides that you can." Turning back to Jay and Lee, she added, " You guys can get the bottles from me in town, I'll be in touch."

She then returned to the ambulance, got in, and drove away in a hurry, spraying sand behind her as she gunned the engine. Lee looked at both of us and at the rapidly disappearing ambulance in a bit of a daze.

"She's in a bit of a hurry, isn't she?"

Jay and I looked at each other and grinned. Doc was well known for having a lead foot and driving as fast as she could wherever she went.

"She always drives like that," Jay replied. "especially when she's behind the wheel of the ambulance. She's scared a few paramedics and a couple of cops with her speed over the years, but she's really good at what she does. And if she thinks we need the FSIU's help, I'll ask for it officially. I trust her instincts."

I just nodded but had to ask. "Where's Hank? I haven't seen him for a few days; I thought he'd be out here with you."

"He got called back to his office after Mr. Pike sent Hugo away and assigned Lee and Judith here."

"OK, I was just wondering. Jay, is there anyone you can call about Mary? Do you know if she had any family or someone close? " Jay just shuddered, "I don't know. I'll look in Sheriff Piggot's files and see if I can find out anything about her, and I'll also ask at the church. So far as I know, she didn't have any immediate family. I don't want to go into her trailer and look. I think I'll leave that for the FSIU. He looked at Lee and continued, "If Doc says they should look closer at her death, I'll believe her, especially if it might be connected to the other craziness around here."

As I stood there, I tried to remember the last time I'd seen Mary, and I couldn't recall. In some respects, she tended to fade into the background, a familiar fixture that you only noticed when it wasn't there.

As we were standing there, I got that prickly feeling in the back of my neck as if I was being watched, and I rubbed the back of my neck, but when I looked at the woods, I couldn't see anything and figured that it was some of the wildlife that was probably curious.

"Looks like you guys are good here; I'm going to take off now; while I'm out here, I just want to check up on a couple of places, then head home." Jay stepped forward, gave me a quick one-armed hug, and told me to be careful.

I was ready to put my feet up, relax, and enjoy my home. The past few days had been scary and frustrating. As much as I loved my mother and father, and as welcome as I knew I was there, there is no place like home.

As I walked towards the truck I was starting to think of as my own, my cell phone rang. I hurried up and answered; I'd been playing phone tag with my insurance agent and wanted to find out how much I would receive, if anything, for my torched truck. I stopped walking for a second and heard, "She was going to talk," and click. Whoever it was had hung up. I did not recognize the number.

I swallowed, took a deep breath, and a chill went down my spine; I turned around, and ran back towards Jay and Lee, who'd been standing and talking. Jay turned around in surprise when he heard me running up to him. I skidded to a stop in a spray of sand. My mouth had dried up at the words and the tone of the voice on the phone.

"Jay, I just got the weirdest call; someone said, 'She was going to talk,' and then hung up." I was freaked between the feeling of being watched at my house, the gunshot, Mary's death, and now this. I was starting to feel like I was living in a nightmare. I'd been so happy to be back home and ready to return to my routine. I just wanted to crawl into bed and just vegetate with this latest call. Lee held out his hand, and I looked at him, but then he motioned towards the phone, and I shook myself a little as he took it.

He looked at me, then ordered 'Unlock it", so I took the phone back from him, did the swipe unlock, and brought back the screen that showed the call particulars, and handed it back to Lee.

"I didn't recognize the number. I thought it was one of the insurance guys calling me to let me know what they were going to give me for my truck, but it wasn't them."

"I'll pass the number on, but I bet it's a burner phone." Lee said with a note of disgust in his voice, looking down at the phone, "You can get them anywhere. " And handed me back the phone,

"Wait a minute, sorry, I'm rattled, but I have an app on my phone that records any calls if I set it up. I've been recording the calls lately because of the insurance stuff; if I don't have a pen handy, I can just listen to the recording, and then I've got it handy. Just a second." With that, I flipped to the call recording app and hit play and speaker on my phone so that Jay and Lee could hear it. Listening to the voice again made my stomach clench. The dead tonal quality in the voice was almost like listening to a computer or something that had no inflection when speaking.

"Send me that," Lee ordered. " I want our techs' to listen to it. Or better yet, give me the phone. I looked at him and shook my head.

"No." I looked at him and continued, "I'll send the recording to you, but no one needs to use my phone to check anything else on it. Give me your number and whoever else needs it, and I'll send it to you and them." I keyed in his number and sent the message to Lee. I'd been watching the sky for a while, and it looked like we would get some weather. The air was also starting to thicken and had a distinct muggy feeling. The clouds had also been steadily clumping and changing color from a lovely fluffy white to the blue-steel gray of an imminent thunderstorm. I quickly looked at the weather app on my phone while I still had it out and could see the red/orange surrounded by green of what could be a severe thunderstorm approaching. "Jay, take a look at the clouds; we're about to get some rain," I called out. "I hope you got everything you need; I think you're about to get washed out of here." With that, I continued onto the truck and left them there. I'd only gotten about 200 yards or so down the road when the rain started. As was usual with the weather here, the rain came in an almost rigid band, I could see sunshine in front of me, but behind me was a solid sheet of rain. I sped up a little; I hate getting caught on the roads here when it's raining. Not only does it get muddy, but because we sit on the sand, if the rain hits hard, it puddles on top before draining away. And it gets slick, and sometimes it gets like wet concrete, which can then catch your tires up and send you sliding towards the ditches that line each side of most of our roads out here. Even with the air conditioning in the truck, I swear I could still feel the humidity in the air. By the time I got home, the rain showers had stopped. I could see where it had rained; there were still puddles in places and on the wet pavement, which was also steaming away. The steaming roads are interesting, especially to people who've never seen anything like them. The roads literally steam when the cool rain hits them.

Chapter 22

As I pulled into the driveway, I was thankful for the latest covering of lime rock on it. I had lime rock delivered and spread out on the driveway every few years. It lasts almost forever, and stays nice and firm, almost like concrete. It makes a great road base as it doesn't break down but gets firmer the more you drive on it. I'd been working on building up the driveway, letting it crown in the middle so that during the monsoon season, I didn't need to worry about water coming up over the road. I wanted it to drain off rather than sit on the road. Hey, it rains down here, and sometimes, it can rain for days on end, and there is only so much that can and does drain away. When I got to the end of the driveway and got the truck turned around, I was ready to climb into bed and collapse.

Skat jumped out of the truck and made a beeline toward her own personal bathroom space. She's a little particular and had claimed one corner of the yard as her own. I never had to worry about stepping in anything nasty, just so long as I stayed away from 'her spot.' I would have to take the weed eater out there every so often and whack down the plant growth. She did an excellent job of fertilizing it. I stood for a moment and breathed in the soup-like air. From the feel of it, we would have more rain coming in. And I knew it was the beginning of our monsoon season. It seemed like Mother Nature just waited until I'd picked the last of the blackberries, and then she decided to start dumping rain on us. It was also the beginning of hurricane season, which meant time to start watching weather patterns more closely. A wave off the coast of Africa could sometimes signal the very beginning of a storm system that could turn into a tropical storm and then a hurricane. It's not my favorite time of year at all. The only blessing was that it usually signaled the end of yellow flies. However, a few diehards always loved to lurk and linger out in the forest and ambush unsuspecting people.

I headed into the house, intent on pouring myself a glass of iced tea; standing with Lee and Jay out in the sun had made me thirsty. It had only been a few hours since I'd been home, but it felt like I'd been gone a lot longer. I hurried up and poured the rest of my cup of tea into a glass, adding a few ice cubes and my usual 1/2 lemon. I do like a little tea with my lemon, and fortified, it wasn't bad at all. I was looking forward to the fall when I could pick lemons again. I hated buying a lemon when I could freeze lemon juice from my Meyer lemon tree and use it year-round. But last year had been a bust for citrus and I barely picked enough lemons to last me the winter.

After draining my glass and letting Skat back into the house, I returned to my little oasis, my back porch, turned on the overhead fan and the other floor fan to get a nice cross breeze, and sank into my favorite chair. I wanted to sit and remember Mary. She'd been a fixture in our town most of my life. Her parents had both passed away, her mother some 30 or so years back, not long after she'd left Mary, and her father about 10 years ago, more or less. She'd cared for her father the last few years of his life as much as she was able. She and her father had understood each other well. I wondered if anyone would mourn her now.

Chapter 23

After Jay told me about Del's mini body farm, I had to admit to being curious. Now that Del had been cleared of torching my truck, I wanted to see what else he'd been up to. We'd kept in touch over the years, very loosely; he had his career, and I had a child to raise. But when I'd run into him in town, we'd always talk a little and even share a pizza from time to time. Sometimes, all he'd do was wave at me from a distance and mime talking on the phone, but it had never happened. I knew he'd had medical issues; he'd confided in me once about his kidney disease, as sometimes when I'd see him, he looked great, and other times, he didn't look good.

After the truck fire and Tate's ambush, Lee had also been sticking close by. He'd also made it plain that he wanted to sit down and talk more about Eric. But I just wasn't ready. I'd told him that he needed to read the letters I'd saved, and then we could talk. He'd changed, but then again, so had I. I wasn't 17 anymore, bedazzled by a young man, and he was no longer the boy who was slightly lost and trying to find his way to adulthood. Lee had also wanted to go out and check out Del's mini body farm, so I said I'd take him with me. I'd found out that Del was home again and cleared it with him for us to come out and look around.

I'd been to Del's place before, but it had been years. Like many of the back roads here, it wasn't paved but did have some road base on it, which helped with the stability of the road. On one side, I could see a drainage ditch, which looked wet. There had been rain after Mary's body had been found at Burnt Bridge, and the water hadn't had a chance to drain away entirely in wooded areas such as this. I was getting ready to turn into the driveway to Del's place when I pulled the truck over. I could see what looked to be churned-up mud to the side of the driveway.

"Why'd you pull over?" Lee asked.

"See the mud to the right side of the driveway? It looks like someone made a turn in there and barely missed the ditch. If you're not real familiar with the way roads are here, you can turn in too sharp and get bogged down in the ditch, especially after a rain. It's more common than people turning too wide. I doubt Del would have done that."

Lee peered through the windshield at the driveway and nodded when he saw what I'd seen. "I see it"

"That usually happens at night when it's harder to see where the driveway is, and someone isn't as familiar with the road. I wonder who was out here?"

"I'm going to call Jay and tell him what you said, just in case." He then pulled out his gun and released the safety on it. After speaking with Jay and telling him about the churned-up mud to the side of the driveway, I put the truck back in gear and pulled into the cleared space in front of Del's cabin. To the left was a woodpile, almost as high as the truck. It looked like the base had been there for years, and there was fairly fresh wood piled up on top. I wanted to leave enough space to back around, so I pulled in close to the woodpile. I hadn't been out here in years. His mom, Ellen, had sold off the family house years before, and Del had kept the old cabin his grandfather had built. This cabin was where he stayed when he came to town. It was a single pen house, much like Tate's house, set up on small bricked piers like many houses here. The older houses weren't built directly onto the ground; they all had a raised foundation. This cabin had stacked and mortared bricks as the pier posts, and there was what looked to be a 3-foot crawlspace under the cabin. The reasons for the raised houses had to do with keeping crawling critters and water out of the houses. Raising the houses also encouraged a breeze under it, which helped to keep it cooler in the summer. Most pen houses had a wide wraparound porch, which shaded the house and also helped to keep it cooler. And like many older homes, it also had a portion screened in, called a sleeping porch. Many people use these, even now and kids love being able to sleep outside, especially when friends stay over. I remembered the old cabin as being a bright white color with bright blue accents on the storm shutters, but it had been obviously repainted and was now a faded light green with faded yellow and pink accents on the steps and around the window frames. The front door had been replaced at one time with side lights being installed on each side and it looked as if it had been really nice. We could see, through the windshield, that somebody had smashed in the front door and glass was all over the place. Lee had just started to say something when I heard glass breaking right behind me, and I got pushed down, and I heard and felt a thunk, and the seat back moved a little. The back window had been shot out of the crew cab. I threw the truck into reverse, heard and felt a bang behind me, and we came to a stop.

 Honestly, the thoughts that run through your mind can dumbfound you. In the space of a nanosecond or two, I'd registered that we were being shot at and I wondered if I'd get to see Eric again, then I wondered what my insurance company would say about me putting in another claim. By this time, Lee had shoved me against the driver's door and told me to get out. I managed to get the handle open and fell out onto the ground.

 Somehow, Lee followed me with not only his regulation gun in his hand, but he'd also managed to get my Ruger out of the glove box as well as my speed loader. I grabbed both from him after hitting the ground. Lee motioned at me to stay down and follow him as he looked around the front of the truck. I'd stopped fairly close to the woodpile, and Lee took off towards it, running and then tumbling behind it to get undercover. I heard a ping and a boom as something hit the truck and did a crouched-down run to get behind the woodpile along with Lee. He handed me my gun and re-loader, and I put the re-loader in my jeans pocket so I could grab it if needed. I'd never shot the Ruger at anyone, the last time I'd shot it I was at the range with Jay, and he insisted that I keep sharp with it. Lee had his phone out and was calling Jay to let him know where we were when another shot smacked into a piece of wood at the top of the pile and showered us with wooden splinters.

He motioned, "I'd like to get away from here. Can you see anything behind us?" Just then, I heard a "psst" and looked over my shoulder and saw Del crawling towards us. He was using his elbows to propel himself forward, much like you see in army training films,and dragging one leg as he crawled towards us, using the other leg to propel himself forward. When I alerted Lee to Del being behind us, he finished calling Jay. He looked at me and motioned to his phone, and I saw he'd not hung up, and the line was still open. I nodded to him that I saw it, and then we both turned to Del, who'd almost reached us by then.

"Thank god you're here," he winced as he motioned to his leg, "Ceb's out there, and he's totally off the rails." He stopped for a second, catching his breath, and continued, "He kicked in my front door a few hours ago and started ranting about how his Dad had hung him out to dry and kept on screaming about his mom letting him down, and that he should have just finished her off." Lee motioned at him to continue, "I tried to reason with him, but then he hit me and I went down, and passed out for a second. As soon as I could, I tried to sneak out the kitchen door, but he heard me and shot after me. It got me in the leg, but I was close enough to the trees and got away. I heard him in the house; he was screaming and yelling and then he got really quiet. I managed to get around here, and then I heard the truck and the gunshots. I wanted to warn you, but I can't even stand up." By this time, Del had gone almost gray in his face, and I could see he was close to passing out. He continued, "He has one of my rifles, I couldn't see which one." He coughed and then passed out. I looked at Lee and tipped my head to where Del had come from, and without saying anything, we managed to pick Del up between us and moved back into the shelter of the woods. We hadn't heard any noise from where the shots had come from, nor did we know where Ceb was. By the time we'd gotten a little further in on the path, I saw the remains of what looked like an old corn crib or something similar and pointed it out to Lee. We got ourselves behind a wall that had been made of stacked logs, pioneer style. I then turned to Del to see how nasty the wound on his calf was. He was wearing the remains of his shirt; one sleeve had been torn off and was currently acting as a pad over the wound on his leg. He'd anchored it in place by tearing the cuff of his sleeve and buttoning it over where he'd been shot. I undid the cuff and pulled the sleeve away from his wound. He'd been shot right above his ankle, and it looked like it had gone right through, looking like it had also hamstrung him in the process. I could see why he hadn't been able to walk. As I carefully replaced his makeshift bandage, Del came to.

"Ceb's a lousy shot, but he managed to get me right through the back of my ankle, hamstringing me so I can't walk. I was running out of the house when he shot me, and I got behind the old Sugaring house. He's scared of the woods here, so he didn't come after me. Dang that hurts," he grunted as I was re-bandaging his wound. Then continued, "I waited a few minutes, then looked at my ankle. I knew I couldn't walk, but I thought I could make a splint using my shirt to tie it together. I bandaged the ankle up, and then I heard a vehicle coming down the driveway, and Ceb started shooting again. I could see the truck, and by the time I crawled over here, you were behind the woodpile. I wasn't about to try hopping over here; even as bad a shot as Ceb is, he would probably have hit me." We seemed safe for the moment, but Ceb was still out there. Lee picked up the phone and started talking to Jay again. I could only hear Lee's side, "We're out behind the house, behind the ruin of some shed. Del's here, but he's been shot and can't walk on his own. "He paused for a moment, listening, then continued, "We can try; I'm sure Del can help us find our way out. " he paused again. "I'm going to hang up, and I'm putting it on silent; I don't want it to ring if you call; we'll meet you out there."

He hung up and turned to us, letting us in on the plan. Before outlining the plan, he asked Del if he could shoot.

Del started laughing, "I grew up here. Everyone learns how to shoot as a kid. I didn't have a chance to grab anything on my way out of the house; I had something else on my mind". I had to shake my head; it was the old Del, a little snarky, and pointing out what to him was obvious.

"Well, in that case, I guess I don't need to tell you how to use this then," Lee answered as he handed Del a small revolver he'd taken from an ankle holster.

"I thought it was only TV cops who had a gun strapped to their ankle," I exclaimed, "so now that we've all got guns, what do you guys suggest we do next? Ceb's got a rifle, and that's got a lot more range than our handguns."

"Jay said if we could make it to where he and Hank got whacked by your bear traps," motioning to Del, "he would meet us there. How far away is it, and how much cover can we get?"

"It's, ummm, just down the trail there, a few hundred feet, but there's minimal cover. I can try to draw Ceb out; he's still a lousy shot."

Lee asked Del, "How can you do that without getting shot again?"

Del had been busy fashioning a splint on his leg, from his other shirtsleeve and a couple of branches laying on the ground. As I watched him, he reached out to Lee, motioning to help him up. As I watched, Del struggled to get to his feet with Lee bracing him. Luckily, we'd managed to get behind the last intact wall of the old sugarhouse, and we could all stand up. Del was white around his mouth and his face was gray with pain, but he was standing.

" If I can get to the corner of the building, maybe I can distract Ceb while you guys run for the road. I used to be a decent shot, and I can try to keep him from following you. There's a trail right behind us here. I've got several cages in the bushes to each side, leading out to the road. You should be able to follow it easily." He stopped talking for a moment to take a deep breath; I could see the pain radiating out from him, then he continued, "I can try to keep Ceb pinned down long enough for Jay and whoever he's got with him to come in."

Lee looked at Del and nodded. "That gun I gave you only has five shots; if Elle doesn't mind, she's got a Ruger and a speed loader for it; maybe you can take it as well. It'll give you a little extra." I nodded my assent and handed Del my gun and the speed loader with the additional bullets. I was relieved; I didn't want to be in a position where I might have to shoot. I'd only shot the Ruger at the firing range at stationary targets.

"I agree; I think you need both guns. Lee's got one, and I don't think I need one just to run to the road."

Del nodded at that and asked if we were ready to run. I looked at Lee and nodded. My heart was pounding, and my mouth was dry from fear. I didn't like leaving Del behind, but he couldn't run and, in fact, could barely stand up. I could see how much pain he was in, just standing, even though he was putting most of his weight onto his uninjured leg. I hadn't realized how thin he'd gotten until he took off his shirt to use as a wrapping on the splint. I could see the bruising on the inside of both of his elbows, where I assumed blood had been drawn for his tests. He also had bruising up and down his arms. It looked as if his body was breaking down. Del nodded at us and asked if we were ready. I looked at Lee and raised my eyebrows to ascertain if he was also ready. He nodded, and I turned to Del and hugged him around the shoulders.

"We'll see you shortly." he nodded and motioned to us to get ready. He hobbled to the corner, holding onto the wall, and holding the gun in his hand he stepped out and shot in the general direction the last shots had come from. A handgun is usually only accurate to around 75 feet but can make a loud noise. As Del shot the gun, Lee and I took off running for the shelter of the woods. Then I heard a crack, and Lee stumbled and fell. It wasn't like anything I'd seen or heard on TV.

    He was actually propelled by the bullet that hit him and landed on his back. I was just behind him and had watched as he was turned towards where we thought Ceb was, the bullet catching him in his right shoulder, spinning him, and making him fall backward. Del stepped out of his hiding spot and fired several shots in the direction the shot came from, which gave us Ceb's location. I finally reacted and grabbed Lee by the shoulders, dragging him back towards the wall we'd been hiding behind. Del let off one more shot and then dropped back towards us.

    He'd been using my Ruger and had emptied the gun. He broke the gun and used the speed loader to fill the cylinder. Adrenaline had been fueling him because he was gray in his face by the time he dropped back behind the wall. By the time he'd finished reloading the gun, I'd pulled Lee further behind the wall of the old sugaring building. Thankfully it had been constructed of thick logs because the barrage of shots Ceb fired towards us just hit the logs, and none penetrated. My ears were ringing from the noise, and it took a second for me to hear Del tell me to pull the shirt away from Lee's shoulder so he could see it. I did so, and my stomach clenched; I was ready to throw up. I could see where the bullet entered his shoulder; the edges of the hole were puckered, and it looked like someone had used an awl to punch through it. I knew what that looked like, as one of Eric's friends had done just that, showing off, when they were teenagers. Del tried to lift Lee so he could look at his back, and I hurried up and helped him. I could feel the blood on my hands; it was disturbingly hot to the touch. I maneuvered Lee up a little so Del could look. I didn't want to look.

"It seems like Ceb grabbed one of my deer rifles. We need to put something on his back to press against the exit hole." He pointed to the shirt I was wearing. "I hate to say this, but, umm, blushing a little, " if you can get your bra off, we can use it to put pressure on the wound in his back." It wasn't time for modesty, but I knew I could get my bra off in seconds without taking my shirt off first. We women can do some amazing things, one of which is taking our bra off without having to undress. I reached behind me, unlatched the hooks, drew the straps down and off each arm, then pulled the bra out from in front of me. I did as Del suggested, looping the bra around Lee's shoulder and across his other arm. As I was getting the bra on Lee, Del ripped the sleeve off Lee's other arm and folded it into a makeshift pad. He placed the pad on the exit wound and used the elastic of the bra to put pressure on the wound.

As soon as we got Lee taken care of, Del collapsed back. As I looked over at him, I could see the sweat on his forehead from his exertion, and that, along with his pallor, scared me. He lay there for a few minutes, panting from his effort while I used my hand to keep pressure on Lee's back. Luckily for him, he'd lost consciousness while we'd been taking care of his gunshot. Lee came to, just seconds after Del collapsed.

"Damn, I feel like a horse kicked me, what happened?" He reached up to his shoulder and discovered my bra, "what is that?" as he felt it.

"When you started for the trees, Ceb shot you in the shoulder, and you fell. I managed to drag you back here, and Del used my bra and your sleeve to put a rough dressing on where you got shot. Del says it looks like Ceb had grabbed his deer rifle, and that's what he's using to shoot at us." As I was explaining it to Lee, Ceb fired a couple more times at us; we could hear the bullets dig into the wood on the other side of the wall. Lee fumbled out his phone, but somehow, he'd managed to fall on it just right, and it had been crushed and was useless. As we were talking, Del came to and sat up.

"Elle, can you see that branch over there?" he asked, pointing to a pine branch that was laying just beyond us, "Could you bring it over here, please?" I dragged the branch over; it was a lot lighter than it looked; it had already begun to break down as much of the branches blown down by wind did in our part of the country. Pine trees would lose branches a lot, and they, in turn, would start to decompose quickly, rot out, and then become part of the soil. Beetles and other insects hurried up the process.

. Just then, Lee put his hand up to his mouth and said, 'Shhhh,' and we stopped moving around. It was then I heard something on the other side of the small tumbledown building we were sheltering behind. It sounded like someone trying to sneak up on us. I could hear the rustling of leaves and vegetation as if someone was scuffing their feet, trying to be silent. There had been a slight breeze moving the leaves of the trees around and the buzz of mosquitoes hovering around our heads, looking for a meal. But now, there was dead silence, with no breeze or insects. All I could hear was the scuffling.

Del had either gotten his second wind or had overcome the pain of his foot because he suddenly jumped out from behind the wall and started firing toward where the shots had seemed to come from.

Suddenly, I heard a thwap, the same sound I'd heard when Lee got shot, and there was Del, on his knees, a gun in each hand still firing one at a time. He'd been hit, but with some weird superhuman strength, he kept firing. And then he fell sideways but still clutching the guns.

I didn't even think this time. I ran out towards him; he'd fallen in such a way that I wanted to straighten out his legs; his legs stuck out awkwardly. I heard Lee calling out behind me, but my whole focus was on Del. By the time I got to him, he was barely breathing but managed to say one thing before he died, and it was a total Del statement said, "I miscounted, I thought I heard six shots.'

I looked to my right and saw Ceb lying down, not 10 feet away. He'd been hit at least twice by Del and was dead. Despite being hurt and balancing on one leg, Del was still a good shot. Lee came out from behind the wall, barely standing, and I could see that he was in a lot of pain and had lost a fair amount of blood as well. It took a few seconds before it registered to me that someone was calling my name, and I looked up to see Jay running toward us, followed by Hank and some other people, none of whom I recognized. Hank elbowed Jay out of the way and reached me first. I suddenly felt a shove from behind, fell into Hank's arms, and heard Nana whisper in my ear, "*he's a keeper."*

"I'd hugged Hank many times in the past, but this time it was different. He held onto me for a few seconds and told me he'd be by later. I'd never looked at Hank as anyone other than Jay's FSIU friend and Eric's good friend. But, after Nana tripped or shoved me into his arms, I had to admit to looking at Hank differently. I also had to admit that the arms that grabbed me were nice and firm, and the brief embrace before he apologized had felt comforting. For just a few fleeting moments, I'd felt safe and protected. I let go, and he moved away, as someone called to him.

The next little while was pandemonium, and I barely registered any of it. Doc Freitag had come and taken care of Lee's shoulder and gotten him bandaged up for now. When Jay and company had gone over to Ceb's body, he had not only Del's deer rifle beside him, but also his .22 rifle as well. It explained the last comment Del had made. He hadn't miscounted; there had been six shots, but one of those had been the .22 that Ceb shot at him or us.

I was finally allowed to leave, Bill driving me home. I wanted to apologize to Bill for the truck being shot up, but I couldn't get the words out. I was exhausted, emotionally and physically. I had no tears and just felt numb. I'd never seen someone die in front of me before, especially a friend.

By the time I got home, I was ready to collapse; all I wanted was to sink into my chair on the porch, pour myself a stiff drink, and then get drunk. I knew it wouldn't help, but I wanted so badly to cry, have a tantrum, throw things, and behave badly. When we got to the house, my mother looked like she was leaving in the car she had parked out front. I figured Nana had signaled that I was in trouble.

I stumbled out of the car, my knees barely holding

me up, and Mom just came over and hugged me.

"Jay called and told me about Del. I'm so sorry. I'm going to go and give his mom a call, but I left you something inside. You'll want to be alone for a while, so come over to the house later. I love you." Turning to Bill she added, "Thanks for driving her home. Elle needs to be alone now, I'm sure you can understand. I'll drop you in town."

With that, she went to her car and waited for Bill. I just stood there, swaying a little but still together enough to tell Bill he could go on and leave; I'd be fine by myself. With that, I went into the house and out to the porch. I heard Mom start the car and leave, and I collapsed into the old Sugan chair Nana always used. I needed to feel her; that was the closest I could come. I swore I felt her hand brush across my forehead, and I heard her tell me to go ahead and let go, but I couldn't, I wanted to cry, but my eyes were dry. I was hollowed out by everything that had been happening in our little town and now Del's death. It was too much. Skat glommed onto me as soon as I came in and lay by my chair. I got out of Nana's chair; even with cushions, I didn't find it as comfortable as my own chair. A bottle of Jameson's and a tumbler filled with ice was on the little table by my chair. I poured myself a double, or maybe it was triple shot into the glass, picked it up, and rubbed the cold glass against my forehead before lowering it to take a sip. As tempted as I was to just down it, and pour more, I sipped and remembered Del, little snapshots of memory, Del as he was when we were young. He never quite fit in, his intellect even then larger than life. He was never a know-it-all but somehow stood apart from the rest of us. The world was less now, diminished and sadder. And I wanted to think about what had happened with Hank; that hug felt different. My mind bounced back and forth between memories of Del and all the times Hank had been there for Eric and me. I had taken his presence at many of the milestones in our lives as just being Jay's friend. I had gratefully accepted that Jay, my father, and my other brother-in-laws had all provided stellar examples of what it was like to be a giving, caring, responsible male. They provided the male influences in Eric's life when he needed it. And when Jay moved back to town, Hank was there a lot. I had thought it was because they were best friends, and it was good for Hank to come here to decompress. But now I wondered.

    Hank had been 'visiting Jay' almost every time Eric had hit a milestone in the past few years. I got up and walked into the kitchen, looked at the brag wall, and saw how often Hank appeared in the pictures of us. Sometimes with a beard, or mustache, longer hair, shorter hair, he rarely appeared with short hair in the pictures. I now recognized that he'd probably come straight from an undercover op, or even during one.

Chapter 24

I'd had a few hours of quiet time when Skat came to my attention and told me someone was on the way down the driveway. She sat there, with her head cocked, listening, and then lay down again. I got up, walked out to the front of the house, and saw my new truck coming down the driveway, Hank at the wheel.

I walked down the steps just as he pulled the truck up and parked it. He got out and walked over to me.

"It looks like you'll need to replace the side windows in the back. If you've got some plastic handy, I can tape them until you can fix them."

I felt a strange unease with him for the first time. But managed to reply, "Any other damage? I know I felt a thunk in the back when I tried to back up, almost like I hit something."

"You've got a couple of dents in the back and a couple of bullet holes. Ceb managed to miss anything vital, but a good body shop can fix it all. I thought you might like to have the truck here, just in case," he said, with a touch of unease in his voice. "Bill's followed me out and will give me a ride back to town." Just then, I heard someone coming down the driveway, and there was Bill. I wanted to say something but needed to figure out what to say. That brief embrace at Del's place had put us on a different footing, and I had no idea how to broach the subject. With a hesitant wave, Hank walked over to the car after starting to hold out his arms for a hug, and then looking like he rethought it and pulled them back. I wanted to hug him but restrained myself as well. Bill had gotten into the car and was prepared to leave. I had noticed he'd looked back and forth between us but hadn't said a thing. I just stood and watched them drive away.

I'd finally been able to sit down and take a breath, or

at least that's what it felt like. There had been so much going on the past couple of weeks that I wondered if life would ever return to normal. Or at least the old normal; I was resigned to having a new normal now. I felt as if I'd been on, not only an emotional coaster ride to hell and back, but I had also weathered stuff I would never have thought of surviving. And I wanted to think about Hank.

Skat, as usual, was sitting as close to me as she could without crawling into my lap. I'd hobbled around the kitchen enough to make a cup of tea and was relaxing in my favorite chair in the living room, looking at the electric fireplace. Nana installed the fireplace just before I came to live with her. She said later that she'd had an idea it would come in handy. I loved sitting there, watching the flames dancing, even when I didn't turn the heat on. Skat was sitting close to me on her little rag rug. She usually sat on it in winter, never when it was warm outside. She preferred to lay stretched out on cool tile during summer. We'd been sitting like that for a while now, me just staring at the flames in the fireplace and letting my mind wander, skipping from memory to memory. Sitting here: rocking Eric when he was a baby and suffering from an earache or a new tooth coming in. Sitting beside Nana in her Súgán chair as she patiently or semi-patiently tried to teach me the intricacies of crocheting. I never did get the hang of crocheting, apart from making doilies.

There were so many good memories, and I was so thankful for being able to sit and enjoy the peace for a little while.

I'd also been looking around the kitchen while my tea brewed; it was modest and cozy, at least to my eyes. From where I stood, I could make out the hulk of the standing freezer in the mudroom I'd bought from a now-defunct restaurant. A freezer I'd been very thankful for many times over the years. With a teenage boy to feed, who often brought home hungry friends, I'd kept it stocked with frozen pizzas, ice cream, and grocery store meat sales. I'd even kept it going during power outages, thanks to the generator I kept in the shed. The old gas stove that kept working even during frequent power outages; I remember an antique dealer offering Nana a lot of money for it once, but she'd refused, as in her words, it works just fine, and why would I buy something new that might not last? I had my brag wall filled with pictures of Eric, his friends, his accomplishments, and a few of Nana holding Eric when he was just an infant. My favorite still was Eric holding a handful of crushed blackberries up to Nana to share. The sheer love in both of their faces, the contrast of the wrinkles on Nana, and the fresh young skin of Eric, his little hand holding that handful of crushed berries up to her mouth, juice dripping through his hand and down his arm. And the dog, a border collie cross, sitting patiently in the background with one long string of drool on his mouth, waiting to clean up the drips. Patches had lived a good, long life before I moved in. He seemed to get a second wind after Eric was born and kept him company for the first four years, and then one day, he just slept away. We then had Gasper, who became Eric's shadow for fourteen years. She had been a dump dog, Nana had found her with a too-small collar, which had almost choked her to death. We'd named her Casper because she was white, could sneak up on us silently, and loved to startle us. However, Eric renamed her Gasper, as she sometimes sounded like she was gasping for air, a legacy of the too-tight collar. She eventually succumbed to a bite from a cottonmouth snake during an epic battle in the yard. The cottonmouth didn't survive the battle either.

    And all the other pictures of Eric, flanked by Hank and me, along with other family members. I'd had my tea and let my thoughts go where they wanted. After looking at the brag wall, my mind went to all the times that Hank had been 'visiting' Jay and had, in turn, shown up for various milestones, major and minor, as well as mishaps in Eric's life. Ever since Hank had brushed past Jay, almost knocking him off his feet to get to me after the shootout with Ceb, I looked at him in a different light. I had never thought of him as anything other than Jay's FSIU buddy. I may have been a single mother, but I had enough adult males in my life who could and did provide masculine influences for Eric. I provided the condoms, but Jay and my father had given Eric' the talk,' And I knew that they'd emphasized courtesy and respect for any girls he'd dated. I knew that because one of Eric's former girlfriends had told me. My son was my joy and not a mistake or inconvenience, but I also was mindful that he was no angel. He got into his fair share of trouble and mischief, and anything I needed help with, I knew I could call on Jay or Hank to help, as well as my father and brother in laws. Eric did not lack any male guidance.

    I don't know how long I'd been sitting, but my cup had been long empty when Skat alerted me to someone coming down the driveway. With all that had gone on in the last little while, I was understandably cautious about who was coming. Skat got up, padded to the front door, and waited.

    The man who got out of the car was Hank. He came towards me hesitantly. Bill had driven him back to town after Hank had delivered the truck out here, and I was surprised to see him again.

    Now that I'd had a chance to catch my breath, I took the time to take a hard look at Hank. His looks were average; he didn't stand out in any way, but judging from the firmness of his body when he grabbed me and held me after the firefight, he didn't feel average under his clothes. I felt some solid muscles in his arms, which I had always noticed in men. Not that there had been many men in my past.

I'd had a few romances. Lee had been my first love. Jerry had come into our life when Eric was around eight and had stuck around for a couple of years, but then he'd followed a long-held dream and moved to the West Coast. Hank had started visiting just after Jay had moved back to town after leaving the city. Which was also about the time Jerry had moved on and away. Not long after Jay became sheriff, Hank started visiting more often. I'd run into him at baseball games Eric played in, and he'd often accompany Jay and Suzanne when they'd show up for various school events. Hank was just there. And I looked at him as my brother's friend. And now he was walking towards me, smiling, and I held out my arms to him.

Chapter 25

Hank

I'd been a part of Elle's life for a long time. She didn't realize it, and neither did her brother.

I'd met her for the first time just after Jay had moved back to Berkeys Corner. I'd known Jay for years before that, but I'd only been there once before he moved back to his hometown. I actually met Eric before I met Elle. I'd been driving into town and saw a boy walking along the road, shoulders hunched and fighting back tears. I recognized the look and the walk. When I saw that boy walking like that, it brought back so many memories. I'd been that boy many times. Walking home after being beaten up for no reason other than we were poor. I think I fell in love with Eric first. When I stopped my car just past him, the boy looked at me almost in recognition,

"My uncle's the Sheriff here, and he knows where I am right now; he's coming up the road ." And he was right; there was a police car coming down the road. As it got closer, the boy's manner changed. His whole body, his shoulders went from hunched over to straight up, and the tears in his eyes disappeared. His mouth, though, was still twisted with emotion.

The police car pulled in behind me, and a familiar voice told me to get out of the car with my hands in plain sight. So I complied and looked up at Jay. '

"What are you doing here?" he asked, "trying to recruit boys now?" as he winked at me. I was known in the bureau as a recruiter back then. In fact, I'd tried to recruit Jay when he first came out of the police academy, after meeting him at Chapel Hill. And he'd turned me down right away. We only got to know each other as friends when he asked for my help, well, the FSIU's help in tracking down a suspected money laundering scheme. Our friendship had progressed until Jay was shot trying to stop a shoplifter, which ended up being an armed robbery. After recovering, he decided to retire early and moved to Berkeys Corner with his wife, Suzanne. I'd visited with Jay and Suzanne several times in the past couple of months. I was under a heavy caseload then, and the time on the road driving brought down my stress load. I'd helped Jay out a couple of times but mostly used my weekends down there to de-stress.

"Nope, just saw this guy walking along the road," motioning to the boy, "and recognized the look," turning to Eric with a nod of my head.

"What's up, Eric?" asked his uncle.
"Nothing."
"Yeah, right? Come on, give."

"It's Miss Maisy; she keeps trying to talk to me about Mom and asks why she didn't tell my dad about me."

"Yup, she likes to do that, doesn't she?"

"Why does she care so much that I don't have a Dad? Mom's all I need, except for you guys and Gran and Pops." he burst out.

"I wish I could tell you. Miss Maisy is a sad lady, though; none of her kids want to talk to her anymore."

"If she talks to them like she talked to me, I don't blame them." said the boy with a head tilt.

Jay then turned to me and introduced us, "Hank, I'd like you to meet my nephew Eric." nodding at me, " Eric, this is my friend Hank," and turned to him and asked," And shouldn't you be on the way to your baseball game right now?"

"I didn't feel like playing today."

"Well, why don't you hop on in the car, and I'll give you a ride," then he turned to me and asked me if I'd like to come and watch a baseball game.

"Sure".

And that was the start. I met Elle at the game, and she seemed nice, but I was there as Jay's friend to watch some young baseball players play a pretty tight game.

After the game, Elle invited us for pizza, and I enjoyed myself. I talked a lot with Jay and Eric, not so much with Elle, but I could see her tight bond with her brother and Suzanne. And it was good to see Jay relaxed and having fun. At the end of the meal, Eric asked me if I'd like to come to another game. They were playing a rival team from the next town, then explained.

"They're going to pack the bleachers with all their friends, and I'd like to have the same," he said, in an adult sort of way. "It's more fun to play when you know you've got lots of people cheering you on." I decided then and there that I'd come for as many games as possible. I had a lot of fun talking with Jay and Suzanne. Elle had stood aside a little, watching the boys play and not talking so much with any of us; her focus was on the game. A couple weeks later, I came down again and watched the game with Elle's entire family there, cheering Eric on. I'd made the time to come and watch their games through the summer until they played for their local championship. Eric had made a habit of watching for me, and on this day, as they won, he'd asked if I would come and stand with them for the pictures being taken. Elle was there, right beside Eric, and he'd maneuvered it so that I was on the other side of him for the picture-taking. As he did many times over the years. OK, so it took me awhile but I finally figured it out, and now now here I was, wondering how Elle would greet me. But I didn't have to worry. As she came out from the back, her arms opened to hold me tight. We walked into the house, holding each other and spent the night talking about everything and nothing.

Epilogue

Life had finally calmed down, at least for the time being. Mom had decreed that she was making dinner and expected everyone to attend, not just the family but everyone else who had helped to solve the murders. She'd laid out tables in the extended sunroom on the side of the house, the one her kids had teased her about wanting because it was so big. But she had the last laugh as it had enough room for her kids, their spouses, and their progeny to sit together.

Walking in, I could smell the rich, tangy spaghetti sauce on the stove. This meal was the fallback, the one Mom made when we all got together. This time around, it was my turn to bring the garlic bread. Each one of us kids took turns bringing the bread, salad, dessert, and appetizer. Mom always made the spaghetti and sauce. Since it was my turn to bring the bread, I decided to make my favorite garlic bread with cheese, one Eric and my nephews and nieces had dubbed 'Elle's Special Bread.' Other people called it a Blooming Onion Bread. It was a perfect accompaniment to Mom's Sgetti Sauce. Which had been simmering for several hours if I knew my mother. No one could hold a candle to Mom's sauce, no one.

Just as I was putting the bread on the kitchen table, the door opened, and in walked Eric, followed by Lee. They were joking and laughing and teasing each other. The lines of strain on Lee's face were almost gone, and I swear I could even see some of the bitter lines disappearing. He looked healthy again and even put on some of the weight he'd lost after being shot. It had been a scary little while with me trying to stanch the bleeding before Hank and Jay had come. Even though Del hadn't made it out alive, I hoped he was at peace, and from what Doc Freitag had told us, after the autopsy, Del might not have lived much longer. His kidneys had pretty much failed, and he couldn't have survived a transplant. As it turned out, Ceb had been behind all the murders, and they'd stretched across the US. Liesle had actually been his first kill, before he tried to kill his mother. Hugo had been a part of obfuscating the evidence and trying to make it look like Del had been the murderer. It looked like Hugo was going to be spending some time in prison, and I and others felt it was well deserved. We could still learn so much, but for now, we were here, and the family was together. Lee had finally read the letters I'd saved for him and the ones I'd written for Eric over the years. And they were now forging a friendship, they'd probably never have a father and son relationship, but it looked like they had started a different kind of relationship.

Jay and Suzanne were behind them, carrying a large bowl of salad. And knowing Suzanne, I knew it was chock full of good-for-you salad stuff. Suzanne was glowing, no longer model thin. She'd put on a few pounds, which suited her so well, along with her belly, which was out front and center and leading the way. After putting the bowl down on the counter, Jay kissed Suzanne lightly on the cheek and told her to go and sit down. Suzanne just laughed, brought her hand up to touch the side of his face lightly, and walked into the living room to join the family gathered there.

Emme and Kay had already brought their contributions to the dinner. Emme and Kyle had brought cheesecake, and it was sitting on the counter alongside some Pineapple topping, both of which had been made by Kyle. He loved to spoil the family with his home baking, and we all looked forward to whatever he made. Kay had brought a big platter of peel-and-eat shrimp along with her special cocktail sauce, which she made a touch on the spicy side.

As I unwrapped the bread, the smell of the garlic

and cheese wafted up and into the kitchen, making a lovely note beside the rich sauce simmering away on the stove. The bread needed a few minutes in the oven to warm up and melt the cheese, and it would be ready to serve alongside the sauce. The water for the spaghetti had already boiled and would be brought back to a boil in just a couple of minutes. Kay carried her shrimp out onto the sun porch, calling out that it was ready, and we all followed her out. Kay makes the best shrimp of all of us. She gets the right amount of heat on them and never overcooks them. Between the adults and the kids and the occasional shrimp slipped to one of the dogs, it didn't take long for the shrimp to disappear.

And then, it was time to cook the spaghetti and serve the sauce. Mom took charge of that, and I got the bread into the preheated oven to warm and melt the cheese.

Jay and Eric called out to Mom to make sure I didn't burn the bread this time. Just because I'd gotten distracted once, and the bread got a little, well we could rescue some of it, but we did have to make a, um, an offering to the kitchen goddess with a lot of it. Charred garlic bread does not taste good at all.

While monitoring the bread, I noticed Mom directing Lee to dish up the sauce. She also supervised Eric as he picked up the colander with the drained spaghetti. She's always been good at multi-tasking and directing everyone involved in the meal. It didn't take long for the spaghetti and sauce to get put on the table, and as they carried it in, I cut the garlic bread into chunks. Hank grabbed the platter and winked at me as he carried it into the sunroom. One of the kids came running into the kitchen looking for the Parmesan cheese, and as I handed him the bowl with the freshly grated cheese, I just smiled. I was home, surrounded by my family, and now we were together and safe. The nightmare of the last few weeks was receding fast. My son was getting to know his father, and they were already getting along well.

And then there was Hank. Life was looking up.

I guess you noticed me mentioning some foods while reading about my adventures. I thought I'd share some of those recipes here.

And in no particular order.

No Knead Rolls.
These are quick and easy to make up, and taste amazing. And they're ready in just under 2 hours. You don't have to bake these in a toaster oven, but if you don't feel like heating up the entire house by using the main oven, these bake very nicely in a toaster oven.
- 2 cups Bread Flour + 1-2 tablespoons for dusting
- 3/4 cup milk, warmed to 120 degrees
- 1 egg
- 1 tablespoon sugar
- 1/2 tablespoon yeast
- 1/2 teaspoon salt
- 2 tablespoons melted butter

Instructions:

1. Warm the milk, add the egg and sugar to it and whisk together. Sprinkle the yeast over top, and wait a couple of minutes. Add the flour and mix in. Then add the salt. This is a wet and sticky dough, so don't be surprised. Cover and let rise for an hour or until doubled in size. I use the bread proofing setting on my oven and let it rise there for 1/2 hour. Punch down the dough, and then separate it into 6 equal portions. I dust the dough with a little flour at this point as the dough is very sticky and hard to handle. Form into 6 equal balls, and place on a greased pan that will fit into the toaster oven. Brush the tops of the rolls with a little melted butter and place a piece of plastic wrap over top. Let rise for

1/2 hour or so, or until the rolls have doubled in size. Turn the toaster oven on to 375 degrees and place the rolls inside. Bake for 15 minutes and if not browning enough on top, turn the oven up to 400 degrees and bake an additional 3-5 minutes. Brush the tops with butter as soon as they are out of the oven. Serve hot.

Candied Ginger and Lime Cookies

1 cup sugar
1 cup butter (2 sticks or 1/2 pound)
1 tsp. Lemon Extract
1 egg
½ Cup Crystalized Ginger, finely chopped
Zest from one Lime freshly zested (1 1/2 tsp.)
Juice from one Lime (1/4 cup)
3 cups good all purpose flour, sifted
1 1/2 teaspoons baking powder
1/2 teaspoon baking soda
1/2 teaspoon salt (if you are using unsalted butter, if not, omit the salt)

Instructions:

Sift all dry ingredients together, and add the chopped ginger and set aside.   If using unsalted butter, add 1/2 teaspoon salt, if using salted butter, omit the salt.

Add the zest and lime juice to the butter and egg. Mix them together and add the butter and egg and let them cream nicely together, just until they are all light and fluffy. I think the extract and the juice added to the sugar helped to break it down quite a bit.

   Continue to mix until they are all incorporated. Then add half the flour, mix and add the rest. You will have a very soft batter/dough at this point. Don't forget to scrape down the sides as you're mixing this together. If you feel it is too soft, you can add an additional 1/4 cup of flour. Take out of bowl, and dump onto a cutting sheet, and divide it into quarters, wrap well. and place in fridge for at least an hour to rest. (anytime you have a lot of butter in a cookie dough recipe, let it rest for awhile in a cool spot, like your fridge. You get lighter and crispier cookies that way.) Preheat oven to 350 deg.

Grab the powdered sugar out of the cupboard and sift onto the surface where you will be rolling out the dough. If you are rolling it out to cut the cookies into shapes.

Take one portion of the dough out and roll out thinly, using enough of the powdered sugar to keep it from sticking too much, and adds a little bit of crispness to the baked cookie.

Cut into desired shapes and place onto a silpat or parchment covered cooking sheet.

Bake for 7 minutes, turn the pan around, bake an additional 3-5 minutes, or until they are just browned a little.

Remove from oven and place onto a cooling rack.

Continue with the rest of the dough until all the cookies are baked.

You can also make a roll of 1/4 of the dough, then cut it into thin even slices and place them on a reusable parchment sheet of paper or parchment paper, on a cookie sheet. Bake for 8 minutes, then take the pan and turn it around and bake an additional 3-6 minutes, or until the edges are a pale golden color.

BTW - the raw dough freezes beautifully and can be sliced almost straight out of the freezer and baked.

Kitchen Sink Cookies-almost Gluten Free

1 ½ cup butter (can use only 1 cup if you prefer)
1 cup white sugar
1 cup brown sugar (I use dark brown sugar, cause I like it, oh and if you don't have any brown sugar, make your own by adding a tbsp. of Molasses to a cup of white sugar)
2 larg eggs
1-2 tbsp. Kahlua (most recipes call for vanilla extract, but I use Kahlua for this, I like the nuance it brings to the cookie, but go ahead and use your own home made vanilla)
4 cups oats
1 ½ cups almond flour
½ tsp. Salt (opt.)
1 tbsp. baking soda
1 cup chopped nuts, walnuts, pecans or whatever you have
1 cup coconut
1 cup craisons or raisins or dried fruit, whatever you have on hand.

Dump the sugar and butter into the mixmaster, or just beat it until the sugar has begun to break down and the mixture starts to lighten a little in color.
Add eggs, one at a time or both at the same time and beat in.
Add the Kahlua at this point, it also helps the sugar break down a little. I like the sugar to be as smooth as possible before I add the rest of the ingredients.
I think it makes for a lighter, crispier cookie. I will take a smidge out and check the batter to see if the sugar has dissolved. OK, so I taste it, but don't do like me if you're pregnant or ill, just in case. It does have raw egg in there. Once that is done, add the oats, almond flour and baking soda, and the salt as well if you use it. Personally I do a lot of salt free cooking and the salt in the butter is more than sufficient for my taste. Next, I dump in whatever I have on

hand, one cup of nuts, one cup of coconut, one cup of dried craisins, or raisins or ... even some chopped up dried apricots, peaches or what ever you have on hand. It's all good.

Using an ice cream scoop, portion out the cookie dough onto a baking sheet, covered with parchment paper. Squash the cookie down a bit, until it forms a flat disk, bake in a preheated 350 degree oven for 15 minutes. The cookies will be soft and need to cool for a minute or so before removing to a cooling rack. I just slide the parchment paper off the cookie sheet onto the cooling rack and let them cool for a few minutes like that. This recipe makes 30-36 good sized cookies.

Rustic Pot Roast

1 lb. Ground beef
1 small onion, diced
1 tbsp. Vegetable or Olive Oil
1 1/2 cups frozen mixed vegetables (more if you like) or 1 can of Vegall mixed vegetables
2 pkgs. Brown gravy mix or leftover gravy
2 cups water
4-6 potatoes, peeled, cooked and mashed, dry
2 tbsp. tomato paste
2-3 tablespoon Butter
salt and pepper to taste
1/4 tsp. thyme (if desired).

Brown meat in a little oil and add onion and continue cooking until the onion is translucent. Sprinkle the gravy mix over the meat and stir in, then add the veggies, after which, stir in the 2 cups of water, slowly, the gravy mix will thicken this. I use some of the water I was cooking the potatoes in. Let it heat through.

Or if using leftover gravy, pour it over the meat and onions, then add the veggies and let it heat through, but don't forget to stir in the tomato paste, it adds a richness to the gravy but you don't taste the tomato.
Pour into a greased oven proof dish, and top with the 'dry' mashed potatoes. When mashing the potatoes, you don't want to add a lot of milk or butter, they should be on the dry side, otherwise they just kinda melt into the gravy, and it's kinda messy.

My trick for getting a nice even coating of mashed potatoes on top of the filling is to dump them onto one of my 'handy dandy' plastic cutting sheets, flattening them out, and then just turning it onto the top of the gravy.

Or you can also make a spatula sized patties of the potatoes and place them on top or you can make the potatoes earlier, let them cool a little and then pipe them onto the meat mixture.

Lots of ways, and I'm just a little fussy cause I hate it when the potatoes kinda fall into the gravy and disappear.

After you get the mashed potatoes situated on top, then dot them with a tablespoon or more of butter and place the casserole dish into a 350 deg. oven for about 45 minutes. Remove from oven and let rest about 15 minutes before serving. Serves 4 people or one adult and one teenager.

Brunsviger (Danish Coffee Cake)

This is a traditional birthday cake for children in Denmark. The dough is made in the shape of a 'Kagemand' Cake man or 'Kagekrone' Cake woman. It's decorated a little with frosting outlining the shapes and with candies sprinkled on top. Personally, I don't do that, I just eat it with as an accompaniment to my coffee. Best served and eaten the same day it's baked, it also freezes well.

INGREDIENTS:

- 4 cups minus 2 tablespoons AP flour (500 grams)
- 14 tablespoons butter (1 stick + 6 Tbsp) (200 grams)
- 2 eggs
- 1 package Dry yeast, 1/4 ounce (30 grams)
- 4 Tablespoon Sugar (4 T)
- 3/4 cup lukewarm milk (2 dl.)

Cinnamon Toffee Topping

- 14 tablespoons butter (1 stick + 6 Tbsp) (200 grams)
- 3/4 cup brown sugar (200 grams)
- 2 tablespoons cinnamon

INSTRUCTIONS:

1. Cut butter into the flour, and add egg along with the sugar.
2. Soften yeast in a little of the lukewarm milk, and add to the dough with the rest of the milk.
3. Knead dough well and roll out into a large sheet and cut it into either a cakeman or cake woman and place on large greased cookie sheet. Mix cinnamon mixture together and spread over the dough. Place in warm place to rise for about 20-25 minutes, bake for about 20-25 minutes in a 325 degree oven. Or place dough in a large pan, spread cinnamon mixture over it and then using the end of a wooden

spoon poke holes down into the dough and let rise for the 20 minutes or so and then bake for 20-25 minutes in 325 deg. oven. Serve warm or cool. Although this is best warm. In fact fresh out of the oven is best.
4. ***Now for my notes on this. I find that when I make this dough, it's too soft to roll out, so I spread it out into the pan with my hands. I use my standmixer to knead the dough. And depending on the humidity and how your flour is I would recommend you sift the flour first.

This was one of Eric's favorite cakes growing up, and is still one that Elle makes on a regular basis for him.

Elle's Special Bread aka Blooming Onion Bread

This cheesy bread is perfect to serve before a game, with some soup, or just because you want a gooey, cheesy appetizer. It also tastes great with Spagetti. And you can always add some chopped garlic to the butter as you melt it.

INGREDIENTS:

- 1 loaf Sourdough or Artisan Bread, day old is best.
- 1 lb. Monterey Jack Cheese, cut into slices
- 1/2 cup melted butter – add minced garlic here if desired.
- 1/2 cup or more, green onion, finely chopped
- 3 teaspoons Poppy Seed

INSTRUCTIONS:

1. Start by cutting the bread in slices, width wise and lengthwise, but not cutting through the base. You want to have some nice little squares going. This can get a little tricky, use a good sharp bread knife to cut it into the squares. Place the bread on a large piece of foil after cutting.
2. Then take a bunch of green onions, and cut them up into a fine mince almost. I cut the onions lengthwise, and then chop them from there. Melt the butter and throw in the onions and poppy seed, set aside.
3. Next cut the cheese up into slices and then cross cut them into small pieces. I forgot to take a picture at this point, so you'll just have to look at the pictures to get an idea of how big to make them. After you get the cheese cut up, you then place the slices in the bread between the cuts. Shove the cheese down as far as you can, in-between the cuts. You really want the cheese to melt into the bread.
4. Then take the bread and place it on a larger piece of

foil, one big enough to wrap around the bread. Stir up the mixture of butter, onions and poppy seed and spoon it over the bread, somewhat evenly.

5. Wrap it up and place it in a 350 deg. oven for 20 minutes, then unwrap it, and turn the heat on the oven up to 375 deg. and let it cook for another 15 minutes or so.

Cocktail Sauce for Shrimp

1 cup Ketchup
1/4 cup Inglehoffer Horseradish Sauce or your favorite brand (use less if you like it milder)
1 teaspoon Worcestershire Sauce
1 tablespoon lemon juice, the stuff in the bottle is just fine here.

Mix together and place in the fridge for an hour or so. This lets all the ingredients get acquainted and at ease with each other.

Cheesecake with Caramelized Pineapple

Topping this light and creamy cheesecake with the caramelized pineapple makes this gluten free cheesecake an exceptional treat.

Ingredients:

Cheesecake

1 1/2 lbs. Cream cheese

1 cup sugar

1/2 cup Agave Syrup

4 large eggs - room temperature

1/4 cup Grand Marnier Liqueur

Crust

1 1/2 cups Almond Flour

1/2 cup softened butter

1/4 cup sugar

Topping

1 can Pineapple rings, (16 oz)

1/2 cup Maple Syrup (add more if needed)

1/2 cup butter

1/4 cup brown sugar

Instructions:

Preheat oven to 350 degrees.

Crust

Prepare the crust by mixing the softened butter, almond flour and sugar and mixing well. It should look nice and sandy. Place a sheet of parchment paper cut into an elongated round and place into the springform pan, making sure part of the parchment paper goes up the sides. Dump the crust mixture onto the parchment paper in the pan and pat it into an even layer around the base and up the sides, keeping it as even as possible. Then, use the bottom of a heavy glass and pack it down. As the crust cooks, the sugar will melt and bind the almond flour and butter together. Bake in oven for 10 minutes. This sets and cooks the crust just a little bit. Take out and set aside to cool while you prepare the filling.

Turn oven down to 325 degrees to bake the cheesecake.

Cheesecake filling

Cream the cream cheese, sugar and agave syrup together until there are no more sugar crystals, then add the eggs, one at a time. Beating well between each egg addition. When all four eggs are incorporated, add 1/4 cup Grand Marnier.

Pour into the prepared springform pan and place on a rimmed cookie sheet and bake in the oven for 1 hour, turn oven off and let sit in oven for an additional 15 minutes. You don't need it browned, and the cheesecake should have a slight jiggle to it when you shake the cookie sheet. Take the cheesecake out of oven, and place it on a cooling rack and walk away for at least a couple of hours. As soon as the cheese cake is cooled, using an offset spatula, run it along the sides of the pan to release the cheesecake. Then undo the springform pan and lift off the sides. You should have a lovely cheesecake. Pull the parchment paper off of the sides, very carefully and trim them at the base. Using the base of the pan, you can now slide the cheesecake onto a serving plate, leaving the parchment paper intact on the bottom, and not leaving the base of the springform pan behind.

Pineapple Topping

Drain the pineapple rings, then cut in half and if you can, slice them in half again, making them thinner or use a fresh pineapple cut into rings, that are very thin. Reserve one ring intact.

Melt the butter and add the maple syrup and brown sugar to the pan over a medium heat. Place one layer of pineapple slices in the pan and let caramelize, turning them after a few minutes and turning them again. As soon as they've changed color, remove to a pan that has sides, cause the sauce will drip. Continue to caramelize the remainder of the pineapple until all of it is done. Add more maple syrup if needed during the caramelization process.

Decorate the cheesecake when cool. Place the whole ring in the middle, then add each half ring around the center, working out to the sides. It should resemble flower petals, a little. Pour any remaining syrup over top and serve.

Mom's Sgetti Sauce

INGREDIENTS:

- 1lb. lean ground beef (feel free to use Ground Turkey instead)
- 1 lb. Hot Italian sausage, removed from casing, crumbled
- 1 lg. onion, diced
- 2-5 Cloves garlic, minced
- 8 oz. fresh mushrooms, sliced or 2 small cans mushrooms
- 3   16 oz. cans diced tomatoes, no salt added
- 2-3 8 oz. cans tomato sauce, or 1 lg. can, no salt added kind
- 3 6 oz. cans regular tomato paste
- 1 can tomato paste with Italian herbs added (6 oz.)
- 1/4 tsp. (or more) red pepper flakes to taste.
- 2-3 tsp. dried Italian Seasoning. To taste
- 1-2 tbsp. Concentrated Tomato Paste – the kind in a tube
- 2-4 tbsp. freshly grated Parmesan Reggiano cheese
- 2 finely grated carrots
- 2 tablespoons Olive Oil for browning

INSTRUCTIONS:

1. Begin by chopping up a large onion, into a fairly fine dice. Throw it in the pan with some olive oil and cook it till it just starts to change color, then add a couple or three crushed and chopped cloves of garlic. Put in as much garlic as you like here. Cook for just a minute or so, and then remove from heat,

and reserve in a separate dish. If using fresh mushrooms, throw them in the pan and just let them cook just for a minute before you add your meat to the pan, brown it and cook until it is no longer pink. Break it up a little with your spatula and then add the onions and garlic to the meat, let it cook for a few minutes more, then add the Italian herbs to the meat mixture. Add some dried Italian seasoning to the meat as you're browning it, this seems to help open up the flavour of the dried herbs. While the meat is browning open up those cans of diced tomatoes, tomato sauce and tomato paste. If using canned mushrooms, go ahead and add them with the tomatoes. Dump the tomatoes into a large pot, mix it up with your spoon until the tomato paste is incorporated and when the meat is ready, add it to the pot. Add in a couple of finely grated carrots at this point as well. Taste it here to help correct the seasoning, and if necessary add more herbs. You can also add a rich full bodied red wine at this point, just a cup or two. Add a few tbsp. freshly grated Parmesan cheese and then simmer for about an hour over low heat, stirring from time to time. (If you have the rind or heel of a piece of Parmesan or Romano cheese, throw it in.) Cook up your favourite pasta, whether it be spaghetti, linguine, or angel hair and serve the sauce over the pasta or however you like to serve it. And it makes a lot.

This is a work of fiction. All the characters and organizations are a product of the author's imagination.

Many thanks:
I want to thank the Writer's Forum for all their wise counsel and being willing to listen to me maunder on about this book for the past few years. I've actually been in the process of writing this for several years and put it aside after my husband passed away.

Thanks to my beta readers, Dawn Radford, Tiffany Howell, Deb Mays, and Lisa Martinez. Your input was invaluable.

Made in the USA
Middletown, DE
03 April 2024